CLAIMED IN THE ITALIAN'S CASTLE

CLAIMED IN THE ITALIAN'S CASTLE

CAITLIN CREWS

MILLS & BOON

First published in Great Britain 2020
by Mills & Boon, an imprint of HarperCollins*Publishers*
1 London Bridge Street, London, SE1 9GF

Large Print edition 2020

ISBN: 978-0-263-08502-0

This book is produced from independently certified FSC™ paper to ensure responsible forest management. For more information visit www.harpercollins.co.uk/green.

Printed and bound in Great Britain
by CPI Group (UK) Ltd, Croydon, CR0 4YY

To the fairy tale heroines
who didn't get to be princesses.

CHAPTER ONE

This door you might not open, and you did;
So enter now, and see for what slight thing
You are betrayed... Here is no treasure hid,
No cauldron, no clear crystal mirroring
The sought-for Truth, no heads of women slain
For greed like yours, no writhings of distress;
But only what you see... Look yet again:
An empty room, cobwebbed and comfortless.
Yet this alone out of my life I kept
Unto myself, lest any know me quite;
And you did so profane me when you crept
Unto the threshold of this room tonight
That I must never more behold your face.
This now is yours. I seek another place.

—Edna St. Vincent Millay, *Bluebeard*

HER SISTERS WERE in a dither.

This was not an unusual state of affairs. Petronella and Dorothea Charteris had never met a molehill they couldn't make into the Alps. Angelina, the younger sister they preferred to exclude from anything and everything, usually ignored them.

But as Angelina slipped through the servants' passageway this evening, racing to change for dinner after another long day of hiding from her family in this petri dish they called their home, she paused. Because she could hear the rise and fall of her sisters' voices a little too well, and they weren't discussing one of their usual topics—like why they were cruelly sequestered away in the family mausoleum as their youth and vitality slipped away…

Because it never occurred to them to leave and make their own way, as Angelina planned to do, when they could sit at home and complain instead.

"We shall be slaughtered in our sleep!" Petronella screeched.

Angelina paused, there on the other side

of the paper-thin wall of the drawing room, because that sounded extreme. Even for the notably dramatic Petronella.

"It will be me, I am sure of it," Dorothea pronounced in the trembling tones of an Early Christian Martyr. Her happy place, in other words. "He will spirit me away, and no. No, Petronella. Do not attempt to make this better." Angelina could hear nothing that suggested Petronella had attempted anything of the kind. "It will be a sacrifice—but one I am prepared to make for the sake of our family!"

Angelina blinked. Dorothea preferred to talk about sacrifices rather than make any, in her experience. What on earth was going on?

Petronella wailed, then. Like a banshee—a sound she had spent a whole summer some years back perfecting, waking everyone round the clock with what their mother had icily called *that caterwauling.* That had been the summer Petronella had wanted to go on a Pilates retreat to Bali with the loose group of pointless women of indiscernible means she called friends—when she wasn't posting competing selfies on social media. Petronella had claimed the screams had nothing at all to do with Papa's refusal to fund her trip.

"Everything is blood and pain, Dorothea!" she howled now. "We are *doomed*!"

That sounded like the usual drama, so Angelina rolled her eyes. Then, conscious that time was passing and her happiness was directly related to remaining invisible to her stern mother, she hurried along the passage. She took the back stairs two at a time until she reached the family wing. Though it was less a wing and more the far side of the once great house that everyone pretended had not fallen into ruin.

Charming, her mother liked to say stoutly whether or not anyone had asked. *Historic.*

Angelina was well aware that in the village, they used other words. More appropriate words. *Rundown,* for example. She had once pretended not to hear the grocer's wife refer to the once-proud Charteris family estate, nestled in what bits of the French countryside her father hadn't sold off to pay his debts, as *"that crumbling old heap."*

Though it had never been made clear to her

whether the woman referred to the house or Angelina's father.

Either way, while her sisters flounced about screaming and carrying on about everything from the lukewarm temperature of their thin soup at lunch to the lack of funds for the adventures they wished to take with their far flashier friends—because they wished to perform it on social media, not because they had an adventurous bone in either one of their bodies—Angelina had spent another pleasant afternoon practicing piano in the conservatory. A room not a single member of her family had been inside in the last decade, as far as she knew. Mostly because there was nothing there any longer. Just the old piano and Angelina, who far preferred the company of Bach, Mozart, and Beethoven to her sisters.

She had nurtured grand dreams of leaving the family entirely and going off to Paris when she hit eighteen. Or anywhere at all, as long as it was elsewhere. But there had been no money for what her father had sniffed and called her "vanity project."

There had been money for Petronella's Year

of Yoga, as Angelina recalled. And for Dorothea's "art," which had been two years in Milan with nothing to show for it but some paint smudged on canvases, a fortune spent on wine and cafes, and a period of dressing in deeply dramatic scarves.

But that was a long time ago. That was when Papa had still pretended he had money.

"Of course there's no money for you to *play piano,*" Dorothea had scoffed. "When Petronella and I have scrimped and saved these past years in the vain hope that Papa might throw us a decent debutante ball. Ironically, of course, *but still.*"

Angelina had learned early on that it was better not to argue with her older sisters. That was a quick descent into quicksand and there was no getting out of it on one piece. So she had not pointed out the many problems with her eldest sister's statement. First, that Dorothea was thirty and Petronella twenty-six—a bit long in the tooth for debutante balls, ironic or otherwise. And second, that there was no point in pronouncing oneself a debutante of any description when one was a member of a rather shabby family clinging desperately to the very outskirts of European high society, such as it was.

Her sisters did not like to think of themselves as shabby. Or clingy, come to that.

Even if it was obvious that the house and family were not *in* a decline. The decline had already happened and they were living in the bitter ashes that remained.

She slipped into her bedchamber, staring as she always did at the water damage on her bare walls. Her ceiling. All the evidence of winters past, burst pipes, and no money to fix it. Her mother claimed that the family's reliance on the old ways was a virtue, not a necessity. She waxed rhapsodic about fires in all the fireplaces to heat the house, no matter how cold it got in this part of France. She called it atmospheric. *It is our preference,* she would tell anyone who even looked as if they might ask. *A family custom.*

But the truth was in the cold that never lifted in this place of stone and despair, not even in the summertime. The house was too old, too drafty. It was June now and still chilly, and the picked-bare rooms and stripped walls didn't help. Slowly, ever so slowly, priceless rugs disappeared from the floors and paintings from their hooks. Family heirlooms no longer took pride of place in the echoing rooms.

When asked, Mother would laugh gaily, and claim that it was high time for a little spring cleaning—even when it was not spring.

The more time Papa spent locked up his office, or off on another one of those business trips he returned from looking grim and drawn, the more the house became a crumbling patchwork of what had once been a certain glory.

Not that Angelina cared. She had her piano. She had music. And unlike her sisters, she had no interest at all in scaling the heights of society—whether that was bright young things who called themselves influencers, who Petronella desperately emulated, or the dizzy heights of the European once-nobles who turned Dorothea's head.

All she wanted to do was play her piano.

It had been her escape as a child and it

still was now. Though more and more she dreamed that it might also be her ticket out of this house. And away from these people she knew only through an accident of birth.

She hurried into the bath attached to her chamber, listening for the comforting symphony of the leaking pipes. She wanted a bath, but the hot water was iffy and she'd spent too much time in the servants' passage, so she settled instead for a brisk, cold wash in the sink.

Because evening was coming on fast, and that meant it was time for the nightly charade.

Mother insisted. The Charteris family might be disappearing where they stood, but Mother intended they should go out holding fast to some remnant of their former grandeur. That was why they maintained what tiny staff they could when surely the salaries should have gone toward Papa's debts. And it was why, without fail, they were all forced to parade down to a formal dinner every evening.

And Margrete Charteris, who in her youth had been one of the fabled Laurent sisters, did not take kindly to the sight of her youngest in jeans and a sweater with holes in it. Not to mention, Angelina thought as she stared in the mirror, her silvery blond hair wild and unruly around her and that expression on her face that the piano always brought out. The one Mother referred to as *offensively intense*.

Rome could be burning in the drawing room and still Angelina would be expected to smile politely, wear something appropriate, and tame her hair into a ladylike chignon.

She looked at herself critically in the mirror as she headed for the door again, because it was too easy to draw her mother's fire. And far better if she took a little extra time now to avoid it.

The dress she'd chosen from her dwindling wardrobe was a trusty one. A modest shift in a jacquard fabric that made her look like something out of a forties film. And because she knew it would irritate her sisters, she pulled out the pearls her late grandmother had given her on her sixteenth birthday and fastened them around her neck. They were moody, freshwater pearls, in jagged shapes and dark, changeable colors and sat heavily around her neck, like the press of hands.

Angelina had to keep them hidden where none of her sisters, her mother, or Matrice, the sly and sullen housemaid, could find them. Or they would have long since been switched out, sold off, and replaced with paste.

She smoothed down the front of her dress and stepped back out into the hallway as the clock began to strike the hour. Seven o'clock.

This time, she walked sedately down the main hall and took the moldering grand stair to the main floor. She only glanced at the paintings that still hung there in the front hall—the ones that could not be sold, for they had so little value outside the Charteris family. There were all her scowling ancestors lined up in ornate frames that had perhaps once been real gold. And were now more likely spray painted gold, not even gilt.

Angelina had to bite back laughter at the sudden image of her mother sneaking about in the middle of the night, spray painting hastily-thrown-together old frames and slapping them up over all these paintings of her austere in-laws. Margrete was a woman who liked to make sweeping pronouncements about her own consequence and made up for her loss of her status with a commensurate amount of offended dignity. She would no more *spray paint* something than she would scale the side of the old house and dance naked around the chimneys.

Another image that struck Angelina as hilarious.

She was stifling her laughter behind her hand as she walked into the drawing room, just before the old clock stopped chiming.

"Are you *snickering*?" Mother demanded coolly the moment Angelina's body cleared the doorway. She looked up from the needlepoint she never finished, drawing the thread this way and that without ever completing a project. Because it was what gently bred women did, she'd told them when they were small. It wasn't about *completion,* it was about succumbing to one's duty—which, now she thought about it, had been the sum total of her version of "the talk" when Angelina left girlhood. "What a ghastly, unladylike sight. Stop it at once."

Angelina did her best to wipe her face clean of the offending laughter. She bowed her head because it was easier and dutifully went to take her place on the lesser of the settees. Her sisters were flung on the larger one opposite. Dorothea wore her trademark teal, though the dress she wore made her look, to Angelina's way of thinking, like an overstuffed hen. Petronella, by contrast, always wore smoky charcoal shades, the better to emphasize her sloe-eyed, pouty-lipped beauty. None of which was apparent tonight, as her face looked red and mottled.

That was Angelina's first inkling that something might actually be truly wrong.

"Have you told her?" Petronella demanded. It took Angelina a moment to realize she was speaking to their mother, in a wild and accusing tone that Angelina, personally, would not have used on Margrete. "Have you told her of her grisly fate?"

Dorothea glared at Angelina, then turned that glare back on Petronella. "Don't be silly,

Pet. He's hardly going to choose *Angelina*. Why would he? She's a teenager."

Petronella made an aggrieved noise. "You know what men are like. The younger the better. Men like him can afford to indulge themselves as they please."

"I've no idea what you're talking about," Angelina said coolly. She did not add, *as usual*. "But for the sake of argument, I should point out that I am not, in fact, a teenager. I turned twenty a few months ago."

"Why would he choose Angelina?" Dorothea asked again, shrilly. Her dirty-blond hair was cut into a sleek bob that shook when she spoke. "It will be me, of course. As eldest daughter, it is my duty to prostrate myself before this threat. *For all of us.*"

"Do come off it," Petronella snapped right back. "You're gagging for it to be you. He's slaughtered six wives and will no doubt chop your head off on your wedding night, but by all means. At least you'll die a rich man's widow." She shifted, brushing out her long, silky, golden blond hair. "Besides. It's obvious he'll choose me."

"Why is that obvious?" Dorothea asked icily.

Angelina knew where this was going immediately. She settled into her seat, crossing her ankles demurely, because Mother was always watching. Even when she appeared to be concentrating on her needlepoint.

Petronella cast her eyes down toward her lap, but couldn't quite keep the smug look off of her face. "I have certain attributes that men find attractive. That's all I'm saying."

"Too many men, Pet," Dorothea retorted, smirking. "He's looking for a wife, not used goods."

And when they began screeching at each other, Angelina turned toward her mother. "Am I meant to know what they're talking about?"

Margrete gazed at her elder two daughters as if she wasn't entirely certain who they were or where they'd come from. She stabbed her sharp needle into her canvas, repeatedly. Then she shifted her cold gaze to Angelina.

"Your father has presented us with a marvelous opportunity, dear," she said.

The *dear* was concerning. Angelina found herself sitting a bit straighter. And playing closer attention than she might have otherwise. Margrete was not the sort who tossed out endearments willy-nilly. Or at all. For her to use one now, while Dorothea and Petronella bickered, made a cold premonition prickle at the back of Angelina's neck.

"An opportunity?" she asked.

Angelina thought she'd kept her voice perfectly clear of any inflection, but her mother's cold glare told her otherwise.

"I'll thank you to keep a civil tongue in your head, young lady," Margrete snipped at her. "Your father's been at his wit's end, running himself ragged attempting to care for this family. Are these the thanks he gets?"

Angelina knew better than to answer that question.

Margrete carried on in the same tone. "I lie awake at night, asking myself how a man as pure of intention as your poor father could be cursed with three daughters so ungrateful that all they do is complain about the bounty before them."

Angelina rather thought her mother lay awake at night wondering how it was she'd come to marry so far beneath her station, which seemed remarkably unlike the woman Angelina knew. Margrete, as she liked to tell anyone who would listen, and especially when she'd had too much wine, had had her choice of young men. Angelina couldn't understand how she'd settled on Anthony Charteris, the last in a long line once littered with titles, all of which they'd lost in this or that revolution. Not to mention a robust hereditary fortune, very little of which remained. And almost all of which, if Angelina had overheard the right conversations correctly, her father had gambled and lost in one of his numerous ill-considered business deals.

She didn't say any of that either.

"He's marrying us off," Petronella announced. She cultivated a sulky look, preferring to pout prettily in pictures, but tonight it looked real. That was alarming enough. But worse was Dorothea's sage nod from beside her, as if the two of them hadn't been at each other's throats moments before. And as if Dorothea, who liked to claim she was a bastion of rational thought despite all evidence to the contrary, actually *agreed* with Petronella's theatrical take.

"We are but chattel," Dorothea intoned. "Bartered away like a cow or a handful of seeds."

"He will not be marrying off all three of you to the same man," Mother said reprovingly. "Such imaginations! If only this level of commitment to storytelling could be applied to helping dig the family out of the hole we find ourselves in. Perhaps then your father would not have to lower himself to this grubby bartering. Your ancestors would spin their graves if they knew."

"Bartering would be one thing," Dorothea retorted in a huff. "This is not *bartering*, Mother. This is nothing less than a guillotine."

Angelina waited for her mother to sigh and recommend her daughters take to the stage, as she did with regularity—something that would have caused instant, shame-induced cardiac arrest should they ever have followed her advice. But when Mother only stared back at her older daughters, stone-faced, that prickle at the back of Angelina's neck started to intensify. She sat straighter.

"Surely we all knew that the expectation was that we would find rich husbands, someday," Angelina said, carefully. Because that was one of the topics she avoided, having always assumed that long before she did as expected and married well enough to suit her mother's aspirations, if not her father's wallet, she would make her escape. "Assuming any such men exist who wished to take on charity cases such as ours."

"Charity cases!" Margrete looked affronted. "I hope your father never hears you utter such a phrase, Angelina. Such an ungrateful, vicious thing to say. That the Charteris name should be treated with such contempt by one who bears it! If I had not been present at your birth I would doubt you were my daughter."

Given that Margrete expressed such doubts in a near constant refrain, Angelina did not find that notion as hurtful she might have otherwise.

"This isn't about marrying," Petronella said, the hint of tears in her voice, though there was no trace of moisture in her eyes. "I've always wanted to marry, personally."

Dorothea sniffed. "Just last week you claimed it was positively medieval to expect you to pay attention to men simply because they met Father's requirements."

Petronella waved an impatient hand. The fact she didn't snap at Dorothea for saying such a thing—or attempting to say such a thing—made the prickle at Angelina's nape bloom into something far colder. And sharper, as it began to slide down her spine.

"This isn't about men or marriage. It's about *murder*." Petronella actually sat up straight to say that part, a surprise indeed, given that her spine better resembled melted candle wax most of the time. "We're talking about the Butcher of Castello Nero."

Invoking one of the most infamous villains in Europe—maybe in the whole of the world—took Angelina's breath away. "Is someone going to tell me what we're talking about?"

"I invite you to call our guest that vile nickname to his face, Petronella," Margrete suggested, her voice a quiet fury as she glared at the larger settee. "If he really is what you say he is, how do you imagine he will react?"

And to Angelina's astonishment, her selfish, spoiled rotten sister—who very rarely bothered to lift her face from a contemplation of the many self-portraits she took with her mobile phone—paled.

"Benedetto Franceschi," Dorothea intoned. "The richest man in all of Europe." She was in such a state that her bob actually trembled against her jawline. "And the most murderous."

"Stop this right now." Margrete cast her needlepoint aside and rose in an outraged rustle of skirts and fury. Then she gazed down at all of them over her magnificent, affronted bosom. "I will tolerate this self-centered spitefulness no longer."

"I still don't know what's going on," Angelina pointed out.

"Because you prefer to live in your little world of piano playing and secret excursions up and down the servants' stairs, Angelina," Margrete snapped. "This is reality, I'm afraid."

And that, at last, made Angelina feel real fear.

It was not that she thought she'd actually managed to pull something over on her mother. It was that she'd lived in this pleasant fiction they'd all created for the whole of her life. That they were not on the brink of destitution. That her father would turn it all around tomorrow. That they were ladies of leisure, lounging about the ruined old house because they chose it, not because there were no funds to do much of anything else.

Angelina hadn't had the slightest notion that her mother paid such close attention to her movements. She preferred to imagine herself the ignored daughter.

Here, now, what could she do but lower her gaze?

"And you two." Margrete turned her cold glare to the other settee. "Petronella, forever whoring about as if giving away for free what we might have sold does anything but make you undesirable and useless. Wealthy heiresses can do as they like, because the money makes up for it. What is it you intend to bring to the table?"

When Petronella said nothing, Mother's frosty gaze moved to her oldest daughter. "And you, Dorothea. You turned up your nose at a perfectly acceptable marriage offer, and for what? To traipse about the Continent, trailing after the heirs to lesser houses as if half of France doesn't claim they're related to some other dauphin?"

Dorothea gasped. "He was Papa's age! He made my skin crawl!"

"The more practical woman he made his wife is younger than you and can afford to buy herself a new skin." Margrete adjusted her dress, though it was perfect already. Even fabric dared not challenge her. "The three of you have done nothing to help this family. All you do is take. That ends tonight."

Angelina found herself sitting straighter. She was used to drama, but this was on a different level. For one thing, she had never seen her sisters ashen-faced before tonight.

"Your sisters know this already, but let me repeat it for everyone's edification." Margrete looked at each of them in turn, but then settled her cold glare on Angelina. "Benedetto Franceschi will be at dinner tonight. He is looking for a new wife and your father has told him that he can choose amongst the three of you. I am not interested in your thoughts or feelings on this matter. If he chooses you, you will say yes. Do you understand me?"

"He has had six wives so far," Petronella hissed. "All have died or disappeared under mysterious circumstances. *All,* Mother!"

Angelina felt cold on the outside. Her hands, normally quick and nimble, were like blocks of ice.

But deep inside her, a dark thing pulsed.

Because she knew about Benedetto Franceschi. *"The Butcher of Castello Nero,"* Petronella had said. Everyone alive knew of the man so wealthy he lived in his own castle on his own private island—when the tide was high. When the tide was low, it was possible to reach the *castello* over a road that was little more than a sandbar, but, they whispered, those who made that trek did not always come back.

He had married six times. All of his wives had died or disappeared without a trace, declared dead in absentia. And despite public outcry, there had never been so much as an inquest.

All of those things were true.

What was also true was that when Angelina had been younger and there had still been money enough for things like tuition, she and her friends had sighed over pictures of Benedetto Franceschi in the press. That dark hair, like ink. Those flashing dark eyes that were like fire. And that mouth of his that made girls in convent schools like the one Angelina had attended feel the need to make a detailed confession. Or three.

If he chooses you, came a voice inside her, as clear as a bell, *you can leave this place forever.*

"He will choose one of us," Petronella said, still pale, but not backing down from her mother's ferocious glare. "He will pick one of us, carry her off, and then kill her. That is what our father has agreed to. Because he thinks that the loss of a daughter is worth it if he gets to keep this house and cancel out his debts. Which man is worse? The one who butchers women or the man who supplies him?"

Angelina bit back a gasp. Her mother only glared.

Out in the cavernous hallways, empty of so much of their former splendor, the clock rang out the half hour.

Margrete stiffened. "It is time. Come now, girls. We must not keep destiny waiting, no matter how you feel about it."

And there was no mutiny. No revolt.

They all lived in what remained of this sad place, after all. This pile of stone and regret.

Angelina rose obediently, falling into place behind her sisters as they headed out.

"To the death," Petronella kept whispering to Dorothea, who was uncharacteristically silent.

But it would be worth the risk, Angelina couldn't help but think—a sense of giddy defiance sweeping over her—if it meant she got to live, even briefly.

Somewhere other than here.

CHAPTER TWO

WHEN A MAN was a known monster, there was no need for posturing.

Benedetto Franceschi did not hide his reputation.

On the contrary, he indulged it. He leaned into it.

He knew the truth of it, after all.

He dressed all in black, the better to highlight the dark, sensual features he'd been told many times were sin personified. Evil, even. He lounged where others sat, waved languid fingers where others offered detailed explanations, and most of the time, allowed his great wealth and the power that came with it—not to mention his fearsome, unsavory reputation—to do his talking for him.

But here he was again, parading out like *l'uomo nero*, the boogeyman, in a crumbling old house in France that had once been the seat of its own kind of greatness. He could see the bones of it, everywhere he looked. The house itself was a shambles. And what was left of the grounds were tangled and overgrown, gardeners and landscapers long since let go as the family fortune slipped away thanks to Anthony Charteris's bad gambles and failed business deals.

Benedetto had even had what was, for him, an unusual moment of something like shame as he'd faced once more the charade he was reduced to performing, seemingly preying on the desperation of fools—

But all men were fools, in one form or another. Why not entertain himself while living out what so many called the Franceschi Curse?

The curse is not supposed to mean you, a voice inside him reminded him. *But rather your so-called victims.*

He shrugged that away, as ever, and attempted to focus on the task at hand. He had little to no interest in Anthony Charteris himself, or the portly little man's near slavering devotion to him tonight. He had suffered through a spate of twittering on that he had only half listened to, and could not therefore swear had been a kind of "business" presentation. Whatever that meant. Benedetto had any number of fortunes and could certainly afford to waste one on a man like this. Such was his lot in life, and Charteris could do with it what he liked. Benedetto already failed to care in the slightest, and maybe this time, Benedetto would get what he wanted out of the bargain.

Surely number seven will be the charm, he assured himself.

Darkly.

His men had already gathered all the necessary background information on the once proud Charteris family and their precipitous slide into dire straits. Anthony's lack of business acumen did not interest him. Benedetto was focused on the man's daughters.

One of them was to be his future wife, whether he liked it or not.

But what he liked or disliked was one more thing he'd surrendered a long time ago.

Benedetto knew that the eldest Charteris daughter had been considered something of a catch for all of five minutes in what must seem to her now like another lifetime. She could have spent the last eight years as the wife of a very wealthy banker whose current life expectancy rivaled that of a fragile flower, meaning she could have looked forward to a very well-upholstered widowhood. Instead, she had refused the offer in the flush of Anthony's brief success as a hotelier only to watch her father's fortunes—and her appeal—decline rapidly thereafter.

The possibilities of further offers from wealthy men were scant indeed, which meant Dorothea would likely jump at the chance to marry him, his reputation notwithstanding.

Unlike her sister, the middle daughter had shared her favors freely on as many continents as she could access by private jet, as long as one of the far wealthier friends she cozied up to were game to foot the bill for her travels. She had been documenting her lovers and her lifestyle online for years. And Benedetto was no Puritan. What was it to him if a single woman wished to indulge in indiscriminate sex? He had always enjoyed the same himself. Nor was he particularly averse to a woman whose avariciousness trumped her shame.

Of them all, Petronella seemed the most perfect for him on paper, save the part of her life she insisted on living in public. He could not allow that and he suspected that she would not give it up. Which would not matter if she possessed the sort of curiosity that would lead her to stick her nose into his secrets and make a choice she couldn't take back—but he doubted very much that she was curious about much outside her mobile.

The third daughter was ten years younger than the eldest, six years younger than the next, and had proved the hardest to dig into. There were very few pictures of her, as the family had already been neck deep in ruin by the time she might have followed in her sisters' footsteps and begun to frequent the tiresome charity ball circuit of Europe's elite families. What photographs existed dated back to her school days, where she had been a rosy-cheeked thing in a plaid skirt and plaits. Since graduating from the convent, Angelina had disappeared into the grim maw of what remained of the family estate, never to be heard from again.

Benedetto had already dismissed her. He expected her to be callow and dull, having been cloistered her whole life. What else could she be?

He had met the inimitable Madame Charteris upon arrival tonight. The woman had desperately wanted him to know that, once upon a time, she had been a woman of great fortune and beauty herself.

"My father was Sebastian Laurent," she had informed him, then paused. Portentously. Indicating that Benedetto was meant to react to that. Flutter, perhaps. Bend a knee.

As he did neither of those things, ever, he had merely stared at the woman until she had colored in some confusion, then swept away.

Someday, Benedetto would no longer have to subject himself to these situations. Someday, he would be free…

But he realized, as the room grew silent around him, that his host was peering at him quizzically.

Someday, sadly, was not today.

Benedetto took his time rising, and not only because he was so much bigger than Charteris that the act of rising was likely to be perceived as an assault. He did not know if regret and self-recrimination had shrunk the man opposite him, as it should have if there was any justice, but the result was the same. And Benedetto was not above using every weapon available to him without him having to do anything but smile.

Anyone who saw that smile claimed they could see his evil, murderous intent in it. It was as good as prancing about with a sign above his head that said *LEAVE ME ALONE OR DIE*, which he had also considered in his time.

He smiled now, placing his drink down on the desk before him with a click that sounded as loud as a bullet in the quiet room.

Charteris gulped. Benedetto's smile deepened, because he knew his role.

Had come to enjoy it, in parts, if he was honest.

"Better not to do something than to do it ill," his grandfather had often told him.

"If you'll c-come with me," Charteris said, stuttering as he remembered, no doubt, every fanciful tale he'd ever heard about the devil he'd invited into his home, "we can go through to the dining room. Where all of my daughters await you."

"With joy at their prospects, one assumes."

"N-naturally. Tremendous joy."

"And do you love them all equally?" Benedetto asked silkily.

The other man frowned. "Of course."

But Benedetto rather thought that a man like this loved nothing at all.

After all, he'd been fathered, however indifferently, by a man just like this.

He inclined his head to his host, then followed the small man out of what he'd defiantly announced was his "office" when it looked more like one of those dreadful cubicles Benedetto had seen in films of lowbrow places, out into the dark, dimly lit halls of this cold, crumbling house.

Once upon a time, the Charteris home had

been a manor. *A château,* he corrected himself, as they were in France. Benedetto could fix the house first and easily. That way, no matter what happened with his newest acquisition, her father would not raise any alarms. He would be too happy to be restored to a sense of himself to bother questioning the story he received.

Benedetto had played this game before. He liked to believe that someday there would be no games at all.

But he needed to stop torturing himself with *someday,* because it was unlikely that tonight would be any different. Wasn't that what he'd learned? No matter how much penance he paid, nothing changed.

Really, he should have been used to it. He was. It was this part that he could have done without, layered as it was with those faint shreds of hope. All the rest of it was an extended, baroque reconfirmation that he was, if not precisely the monster the world imagined him, a monster all the same.

It was the hope that made him imagine otherwise, however briefly.

This was not the first time he'd wished he could excise it with his own hands, then cast it aside at last.

The house was not overly large, especially with so much of it unusable in its current state, so it took no time at all before they reached the dining room on the main floor. His host offered an unctuous half bow, then waved his arm as if he was an emcee at a cabaret. A horrifying notion.

Benedetto prowled into the room, pleased to find that this part of the house, unlike the rest with its drafts and cold walls despite the season, was appropriately warm.

Perhaps too warm, he thought in the next moment. Because as he swept his gaze across the room, finding the oldest and middle daughter to be exactly as he'd expected, it was as if someone had thrown gas on a fire he could not see. But could feel inside of him, cranked up to high.

The flames rose higher.

He felt scalded. But what he saw was an angel.

Angelina, something in him whispered.

For it could be no other.

Her sisters were attractive enough, but he had already forgotten them. Because the third, least known Charteris daughter stood next to her mother along one side of a formally set table, wearing a simple dress in a muted hue and a necklace of complicated pearls that seemed to sing out her beauty.

But then, she required no embellishment for that. She was luminous.

Her hair was so blond it shone silver beneath the flickering flames of a chandelier set with real candles. Economy, not atmosphere, he was certain, but it made Angelina all the more lovely. She'd caught the silvery mass back at the nape of her neck in a graceful chignon that he longed to pick apart with his hands. Her features should have been set in marble or used to launch ships into wars. They made him long to paint, though he had never wielded a brush in all his days.

But he thought he might learn the art of oils against canvas for the express purpose of capturing her. Or trying. Her high cheekbones, her soft lips, her elegant neck.

He felt his heart, that traitorous beast, beat too hard.

"Here we all are," said Anthony Charteris, all but chortling with glee.

And in that moment, Benedetto wanted to do him damage. He wanted to grab the man around his portly neck and shake him the way a cat shook its prey. He wanted to make the man think about what it was he was doing here. Selling off a daughter to a would-be groom with a reputation such as Benedetto's? Selling off an angel to a devil, and for what?

But almost as soon as those thoughts caught at him, he let them go.

Each man made his own prison. His own had contained him for the whole of his adult life and he had walked inside, turned the key, and fashioned his own steel bars. Who was he to cast stones?

"This is Benedetto Franceschi," Charteris announced, and then frowned officiously at his daughters. "He is a very important friend and business partner. *Very* important."

Some sort of look passed between the man and his wife. Margrete, once a Laurent, drew herself up—no doubt so she could present her bosom to Benedetto once more. Then again, perhaps that was how she communicated.

He remained as he had been before: vaguely impressed, yet unmoved.

"May I present to you, sir, my daughters." Margrete gestured across the table. "My eldest, Dorothea." Her hand moved to indicate the sulky, too self-aware creature beside the eldest, who smirked a bit at him as if he had already proposed to her. "My middle daughter, Petronella."

And at last, she indicated his angel. The most beautiful creature Benedetto had ever beheld. His seventh and last wife, God willing. "And this is my youngest, Angelina."

Benedetto declared himself suitably enchanted, waited for the ladies to seat themselves, and then dropped into his chair with relief. Because he wanted to concentrate on Angelina, not her sisters.

He wanted to dispense with this performance. Announce that he had made his choice and avoid having to sit through an awkward meal like this one, where everyone involved was pretending that they'd never heard of the many things he was supposed to have done. Just as he was pretending he didn't notice that the family house was falling down around them as they sat here.

"Tell me." Benedetto interrupted the meaningless prattle from Charteris at the head of the table about his ancestors or the Napoleonic Wars or some such twaddle. "What is it you do?"

His eyes were on the youngest daughter, though she had not once looked up from her plate.

But it was the eldest who answered, after clearing her throat self-importantly. "It is a tremendous honor and privilege that I get to dedicate my life to charity," she proclaimed, a hint of self-righteousness flirting with the corners of her mouth.

Benedetto had many appetites, but none of them were likely to be served by the indifferent food served in a place like this, where any gesture toward the celebrated national cuisine had clearly declined along with the house and grounds. He sat back, shifting his attention from the silver-haired vision to her sister.

"And what charity is it that you offer, exactly?" he asked coolly. "As I was rather under the impression that your interest in charity ball attendance had more to do with the potential of fetching yourself a husband of noble blood than any particular interest in the charities themselves."

Then he watched, hugely entertained, as Dorothea flushed. Her mouth opened, then closed, and then she sank back against her seat without saying a word. As if he'd taken the wind out of her sails.

He did tend to have that effect.

The middle daughter was staring at him, so Benedetto merely lifted a brow. And waited for her to leap into the fray.

Petronella did not disappoint. Though she had the good sense to look at him with a measure of apprehension in her eyes, she also propped her elbows on the table and sat forward in such a way that her breasts pressed against the bodice of the dress she wore. An invitation he did not think was the least bit unconscious.

"I consider myself an influencer," she told him, her voice a husky, throaty rasp that was itself another invitation. All of her, from head to toe, was a carefully constructed beckoning. She did not smile at him. She kept her lips in what appeared to be a natural pout while gazing at him with a directness that he could tell she'd practiced in the mirror. Extensively.

"Indeed." His brow remained where was, arched high. "What influence do you have? And over what—or whom?"

"My personal brand is really a complicated mix of—"

"I am not interested in brands," Benedetto said, cutting her off. "Brands are things that I own and use at will according to my wishes. The purpose of a brand is to sell things. Influence, on the other hand, suggests power. Not the peddling of products for profit. So. What power do you have?"

She shifted in her chair, a strange expression on her face. It took him a moment to recognize it as false humility. "I couldn't possibly say why some people think I'm worth listening to," she murmured.

Benedetto smiled back, and enjoyed watching the unease wash over her as he studied her, because he was more the monster they thought he was than he liked to admit.

Especially in polite company.

"Pretty is not power," he said softly. "Do you know how you can tell? Because men wish to possess it, not wield it. It is no different from any other product, and like them, happily discarded when it outgrows its usefulness or fades in intensity. Surely you must know this."

Petronella, too, dropped her gaze. And looked uncertain for the first time since Benedetto had walked in to the dining room.

He was not the least bit surprised that neither of the Charteris parents intervened. Parents such as these never did. They were too wrapped up in what they had to gain from him to quibble over his harshness.

But he hardly cared because, finally, he was able to focus on the third daughter. The aptly named Angelina.

"And you?" he asked, feeling a coiling inside of him, as if he was some kind of serpent about to strike. As if he was every bit the monster the world believed he was. "What is it you do?"

"Nothing of consequence," she replied.

Unlike her sisters, Angelina did not look up from her plate, where she was matter-of-factly cutting into a piece of meat he could see even from where he sat was tough. They had given the choice cuts to him and to themselves, of course. Letting their children chew on the gristle. That alone told him more than he needed to know about the Charteris family. About their priorities.

Perhaps the truth no one liked to face was that some people deserved to meet a monster at the dinner table.

"Angelina," bit out Margrete, in an iron voice from behind a pasted-on smile and that magnificent chest like the prow of a ship.

"I spoke the truth," Angelina protested.

But she placed her cutlery down, very precisely. She folded her hands in her lap. Then she raised her gaze to Benedetto's at last. He felt the kick of it, her eyes blue and innocent and dreamy, like the first flush of a sweet spring.

"I play the piano. Whenever I can, for as long as I can. My other interests include listening to other people play the piano on the radio, taking long walks while thinking about how to play Liszt's *La Campenella* seamlessly, and reading novels."

Her voice was not quite insolent. Not *quite*. Next to her, her mother drew herself up again, as if prepared to mete out justice—possibly in the form of a sharp slap, if Benedetto was reading the situation correctly—but he lifted a hand.

"Both of your sisters attempt to interact with the outside world. But not you. There's no trace of you on the internet, for example, which is surpassingly strange in this day and age."

There was heat on her cheeks. A certain glitter in her gaze that made his body tighten.

"There are enough ways to hide in a piece of music," she said after a moment stretched thin and filled with the sounds of tarnished silver against cracked china. “Or a good book. Or even on a walk, I suppose. I have no need to surrender myself to still more ways to hide myself away, by curating myself into something unrecognizable.”

Petronella let out an affronted sniff, but Angelina did not look apologetic.

“Some would say that it is only in solitude that one is ever able to stop hiding and find one’s true self,” Benedetto said.

And did not realize until the words were out there, squatting in the center of the silent table, how deeply felt that sentiment was. Or was that merely what he told himself?

“I suppose that depends.” And when Angelina looked at him directly then, he felt it like an electric charge. And more, he doubted very much that she’d spent any time at all practicing her expression in reflective glass. “Are you speaking of solitude? Or solitary confinement? Because I don’t think they’re the same thing.”

“No one is speaking about solitary confinement, Angelina,” Margrete snapped, and Benedetto had the sudden, unnerving sensation that he'd actually forgotten where he was. That for a moment, he had seen nothing but Angelina. As if the rest of the world had ceased to exist entirely, and along with it his reality, his responsibilities, his fearsome reputation, and the reason he was here…

Pull yourself together, he ordered himself.

The dinner wore on, course after insipid course. Anthony and Margrete filled the silence, chattering aimlessly, while Benedetto seethed. And the three daughters who were clearly meant to vie for his favor stayed quiet, though he suspected that the younger one kept a still tongue for very different reasons than her sisters.

"Well," said Anthony with hearty and patently false bonhomie, when the last course had been taken away untouched by a surly maid. "Ladies, why don't you repair to the library while Signor Franceschi and I discuss a few things over our port."

So chummy. So pleased with himself.

"I think not," Benedetto said, decisively, even as the older daughters started to push back their chairs.

At the head of the table, Anthony froze.

Benedetto turned toward Angelina, who tensed—almost as if she knew what he was about to say. "I wish to hear you play the piano," he said.

And when no one moved, when they all gazed back at him in varying degrees of astonishment, outright panic, and pure dislike, he smiled.

In the way he knew made those around him…shudder.

Angelina stared back at him in something that was not quite horror. "I beg your pardon?"

Benedetto smiled wider. "Now, please."

CHAPTER THREE

"ALONE," ADDED THE TERRIBLE, notorious man when Angelina's whole family made as if to rise.

He smiled all the while, in a manner that reminded Angelina of nothing so much as the legends she'd heard all her life about men who turned into wolves when the moon was high. She was tempted to run to the windows and see what shape the moon took tonight, though she did not dare.

And more, could not quite bring herself to look away from him.

Angelina had not been prepared for this. For him.

It was one thing to look at photographs. But there was only so much raw magnetism a person could see on the screen.

Because in person, Benedetto Franceschi

was not merely beautiful or sinful, though he was both.

In person, he was volcanic.

Danger simmered around him, charging the air, making Angelina's body react in ways she'd thought only extremes of temperatures could cause. Her chest felt tight, hollow and too full at once, and she found it almost impossible to take a full breath.

When he'd singled her out for conversation she'd responded from her gut, not her head. And knew she'd handled it all wrong, but only because of her mother's reaction. The truth was, her head had gone liquid and light and she'd had no earthly idea what had come out of her mouth.

Nothing good, if the pinched expression on Margrete's face was any guide.

Still, disobedience now did not occur to her. Not because she feared her parents, though she supposed that on some level, she must. Or why would she subject herself to this? Why would she still be here? But she wasn't thinking of them now.

Angelina wasn't thinking at all, because

Benedetto's dark, devil's gaze was upon her, wicked and insinuating. A dare and an invitation and her own body seemed to have turned against her.

He wanted to hear her play.

But a darker, less palatable truth was that she wanted to play for him.

She told herself it was only that she wanted an audience. Any audience. Yet the dark fire of his gaze worked its way through her and she knew she wasn't being entirely honest. The yearning for an audience, instead of the family members who ignored her, wasn't why her pulse was making such a racket, and it certainly wasn't why she could feel sensation hum deep within her.

She could hardly breathe and yet she stood. Worse, she knew that she *wanted* to stand. Then she turned, leading him out of the dining chamber, careful not to catch her sisters' eyes or sneak a glance at her worryingly, thunderously quiet father on her way out.

Angelina tried to steel herself against him as she moved through the murky depths of the house, certain that he would try to speak to her the moment they were alone. Charm her into unwariness or attempt to disarm her with casual conversation.

But instead, he walked in silence.

And that was much, much worse.

She was so aware of him it made her bones ache. And it took only a few steps to understand that her awareness of him was not based on fear. Her breasts and her belly were tight, and grew tighter the farther away they moved from the dining room. Deep between her legs she felt swollen, pulsing in time with her heart as it beat and beat.

Helpless. Hopeless.

Red hot and needy.

The house brought it all into sharp relief. It was dimly lit and echoing, so that their footsteps became another pulse, following them. Chasing them on. Angelina was certain that if she looked at the shadow he cast behind them, she would see not a man, but a wolf.

Fangs at the ready, prepared to attack.

She could not have said why that notion made her whole body seem to boil over, liquid and hot.

She walked on and on through a house that seemed suddenly cavernous, her mind racing and spinning. Yet she couldn't seem to grasp on to a single thought, because she was entirely too focused on the man beside her and slightly behind her, matching his stride to hers in a way that made her feel dirty, somehow.

It felt like a harbinger. A warning.

She was relieved when they reached the conservatory at last, and for once didn't care that it was more properly an abandoned sunroom. She rushed inside, shocked to see that her hands trembled in the light from the hall as she picked up the matches from the piano bench, then set about lighting the candles on the candelabra that sat atop her piano.

Because her parents only lit a portion of the house, and this room only Angelina used did not qualify.

But then it was only the two of them in the candlelight, and that made the pulse in her quicken. Then drum deep.

Especially when, overhead through the old glass, she could see the moon behind the clouds—a press of light that did not distinguish itself enough for her to determine its shape. Or fullness.

Angelina settled herself on the piano bench. And it took her a moment to understand that it wasn't her pulse that she could hear, seeming to fill the room, but her own breathing.

Meanwhile, Benedetto stood half in shadow, half out. She found herself desperately trying to see where the edges of his body ended and the shadows began, because it seemed to her for a panicked moment there that there was no difference between the two. That he was made of shadows and inky dark spaces, and only partly of flesh and bone.

"We have electricity," she felt compelled to say, though her voice felt like a lie on her tongue. Too loud, too strange, when his eyes were black as sin and lush with invitation. Everything in her quivered, but she pushed on. "My parents encourage us to keep things more…atmospheric."

"If you say so."

His voice was another dark, depthless shadow. It moved in her, swirling around and around, making all the places where she pulsed seem brighter and darker at once.

She sat, breathing too heavily, her hands curved above the smooth, worn keys of this instrument that—some years—had been her only friend.

"What do you want me to play?"

"Whatever you like."

She did not understand how he could say something so innocuous and leave her feeling as if that mouth of his was moving against her skin, leaving trails all over her body, finding those places where she already glowed with a need she hardly recognized.

You recognize it, something in her chided her. *You only wish you didn't.*

Angelina felt misshapen. Powerful sensations washed over her, beating into her until she felt as if she might explode.

Or perhaps the truth was that she wanted to explode.

She spread her hands over the keys, waiting for that usual feeling of rightness. Of coming home again. Usually this was the moment where everything felt right again. Where she found her hope, believed in her future, and could put her dreary life aside. But tonight, even the feel of the ivory beneath her fingers was a sensual act.

And somehow his doing.

"Are you afraid of me, little one?" Benedetto asked, and his voice seemed to come from everywhere at once. From inside her. From deep between her legs. From that aching hunger that grew more and more intense with every second.

She shifted on the bench. Then she stared at him, lost almost instantly in his fathomless gaze. In the dark of the room with the night pressing down outside. In the flickering candlelight that exposed and concealed them both in turn.

Angelina felt as if she was free falling, tumbling from some great height, fully aware that when she hit the ground it would break her—but she couldn't look away.

She didn't *want* to look away.

He was the most marvelous thing that had ever happened to her, even if he really was a murderer.

She didn't know where to put that.

And again, she could hear her own breath. He leaned against the side of the piano, stretching a hand out across the folded back lid, and her eyes followed the movement. Compulsively. As if she had no choice in the matter.

She would have expected a man so wealthy and arrogant to have hands soft and tender like the belly of a small dog. She wouldn't have been surprised to see a careful manicure. Or a set of garish rings.

But his hand was bare of any accoutrement. And it was no tender, soft thing. It looked tough, which struck her as incongruous even as the notion moved in her like heat. His fingers were long, his palms broad.

And she could not seem to keep herself from imagining them touching her skin, cupping her breasts, gripping her bottom as he pulled her beneath him and made her his.

When a different sound filled the room, she understood that she'd made it. She'd gasped. Out loud. And that darkness he wore too easily seemed to light up with a new kind of fire she couldn't read.

"I'm accustomed to having my questions answered," he said in a quiet tone, but all she heard was menace.

And she had already forgotten the question, and possibly herself. So she did the only thing she could under the circumstances.

Angelina began to play.

She played and she played. She played him melodies that spoke of her dreams, her hopes, and then the crushing storm of her father's losses. She played him stories of her confinement here and the bitter drip of years in this ruined, forgotten place. Then she played him songs that felt like he did, impossible and terrifying and thrilling all the same.

She felt caught in the grip of his unwavering, relentless gaze. And the notes that crashed all around them, holding them tight even as they sang out the darkest, most hidden parts of her.

And while she played, Angelina found she couldn't lose herself the way she usually did.

Instead, it was as if she was found. As if

he had found her here, trapping her and exalting her at once.

So she played that, too.

She played and played, until he stepped out of the shadows and his face was fully in the candlelight.

Fierce. Haunted. Sensual.

And suffused with the same rich, layered hunger she could feel crashing around inside of her.

For a long time, while the music danced from her fingers into the keys and then filled the room, it was as if she couldn't tell which one of them was which. His hands did not touch her body, and yet somehow they were all over her. She could feel the scrape of his palm, the stirring abrasion of his calloused fingers.

And she explored him, too, with every note she coaxed from her piano. They were tossed together in the melody, tangled, while the music tied them in knots and made them one glorious note, held long and pure—

When she stopped playing, for a moment she couldn't tell the difference.

And then the next, his hands were on her.

His beautiful, terrible hands, for real this time.

He sank his fingers into her hair, pulling it from her chignon—and not gently. And her whole body seemed to bloom. His face was over hers, his mouth as grim as his eyes were hot. And then he bent her back at an angle that should have alarmed her, but instead sent a thick delight storming through her in every direction.

He feasted on her neck like the wolf she half imagined he was, teasing his way around those sullen, moody pearls she wore.

I need, she thought, though she could not speak.

The more he tasted her flesh, the more she felt certain that he stole her words. That as his mouth moved over her skin, he was altering her.

Taking her away from here. From herself. From everything she knew.

He shifted then, spreading her out on the piano bench. She lay down where he put her, grateful to have the bench at her back. Then he lowered himself over her, the dark bespoke suit he wore seeming blacker than pitch in the candlelight. He skimmed his wicked hands down the length of her body, moving his way down until he wrenched the skirt of her shift dress up to her waist.

It didn't occur to her to object.

Not when every part of her wanted to sing out instead, glory and hope alike, and no matter that this man was not safe. There was no safety in staying where she was, either. There was only disappointment and the slow march of tedious years, and Benedetto felt like an antidote to that.

He touched her and she felt as if she was the piano, and he was making her a melody.

She threw her arms over her head and arched into him.

Then she felt his mouth, again. She heard his dark laugh, desire and delight. He tasted the tender flesh of her inner thigh and she could not have described the sounds she made. She could only *feel* them, coming out of her like an echo of those same songs she'd played for him.

When she could feel the harsh beauty of them in her fingers, she realized that she was gripping his strong shoulders instead.

"Angelina," he said, there against her thigh where she could feel her own name like a brand against her skin. In the candlelight that danced and flickered, she lifted her head and found herself lost in his gaze with only her own body between them. "Are you afraid of me?"

"Yes," she lied.

He laughed, a rich, dark sound that crashed over her like a new symphony, louder and more tumultuous by far.

Then he shifted, pulled her panties to one side, and licked deep into the center of her need.

And then Benedetto Franceschi, the Butcher of Castello Nero, ate her alive.

He made her scream.

She bucked against him, crying out for deliverance but receiving nothing but the slide of his tongue, the faint scrape of his teeth. A benediction by any measure.

And when she died from the pleasure of

it—only to find she lived somehow after all, shuddering and ruined and shot through with some kind of hectic glee—he pulled her to her feet, letting her shift dress do what it would. He sank his hands into her hair again, and then this time, he took her mouth with his.

Sensation exploded in her all over again, hotter and wilder this time.

The madness of these melodies. The glorious terror of his possession.

The dark marvel of it all.

His mouth had been between her legs, and the knowledge of that made her shake all over again. She pulsed and shook, and she was too inexperienced to know what part of the rough, intoxicating taste was him, and which part her.

So she angled her head and met him as he devoured her.

Angelina felt debauched and destroyed. As ruined as this house they stood in.

And why had she never understood that the real price of a ruin like this was the sheer joy in it?

The dark, secret joy that coursed through her veins, pooled between her legs, and made her arch against him as if all this time, all these years, her body had been asleep. Only now had it woken up to its true purpose.

Here. With him.

Like this.

He kissed her and he kissed her.

When he finally lifted his mouth from hers, his grin was a ferocious thing. Angelina felt it inside her, as if she was made fierce, too, because of him.

And she had never known, until this moment, how deeply she wanted to be fierce.

"If you marry me," he told her, in that dark, intense voice of his, "you can never return here. You will no more be a part of your family. You will belong to me and I am a jealous, possessive creature at the best of times. I do not share what is mine."

Angelina hardly felt like herself. There was too much sensation coursing in her and around her, she couldn't tell if it was the music she'd played or the way he'd played her body in turn, but she couldn't seem to worry about that the way she should.

The way a wiser woman would have, with a man like him.

"Is that a warning or promise?" she asked instead.

"It is a fact."

And her skirt was still rucked up. She felt uncomfortably full in the bodice of her dress. She could not tell which was more ravaged and alight, the aching center of her need between her legs or her mouth.

But the candlelight made all of that seem unimportant.

Or perhaps, whispered a voice inside her, *it is not the light that seduces you, but the dark that makes it shine.*

"If I marry you," she said, because she was already ruined, and she wanted things she was afraid to name, "I want to live. I don't want to die."

And then, for the first time since they'd walked away from her family and into this chilly, barren room, it occurred to her to worry about the fact that he was a man with six dead wives. She was all alone with him and everyone believed he was a murderer.

Why did something in her want to believe otherwise?

His mouth was a bitter slash. His eyes were much too dark.

For the first time, Angelina wanted to cover herself. She felt cold straight through.

If she could have taken the words back, she would have. If she could have kept him from touching her, she—

But no. Whatever happened next, his mouth on her had been worth it.

"Every one of us must die, little one," Benedetto said, his voice a mere thread of sound. It wound through her and then flowered into something far richer and more textured than fear, making Angelina shudder as if he was licking into her molten core again. "But we will do so in the way we live, like it or not. That I can promise you."

CHAPTER FOUR

A MONTH LATER, Angelina woke up to the sound of hammering, the way she had almost every morning since that first night.

The only difference was that today was her wedding day, like it or not.

Construction on the old house had begun immediately. Benedetto had made good on his promise with crews arriving by truck-load at first light. Since then, day after day, the hammering fused with that pulse inside her, until she couldn't tell whether her heart beat inside or outside of her body.

It had been the longest and shortest month of her life.

Her sisters veered between something like outrage and a more simple, open astonishment. And sometimes, when they remembered themselves, a surprising show of concern.

"You must be careful," Petronella had said very seriously, one evening. She'd come and interrupted Angelina in the conservatory, where Angelina played piece after piece as if the piano was telling stories to keep her alive. And as long as she played she would be safe. Night after night, she played until her fingers cramped, but nothing eased that ravaged, misshapen feeling inside of her. "Whatever happens, and whatever he does to you in that castle of his, you must not react."

"I didn't think you knew where the conservatory was." Angelina blinked at her sister in the flickering candlelight. Outside, a bloated summer moon rose over the trees. "Are you lost?"

"I'm serious, Angelina," Petronella snapped, scowling, which felt more like her sister than this strange appearance and stab at worry. "One dead wife could be an accident. The second could be a terrible tragedy. I could even *maybe* think that a third might be a stroke of very bad luck indeed. But six?"

Angelina slammed her hands on the keys, the discordant jangle of noise sounding a great deal like she felt inside. As if her ribs were piano keys she'd forgotten how to play.

Maybe that was what getting married was supposed to feel like.

"I don't need you to remind me who he is," she said.

Another slap of noise.

Petronella looked different in the candlelight. Younger. Softer. She lifted her hand, almost as if she intended to reach over and stroke Angelina with it. But she thought better of it, or the urge passed, and she dropped it to her side.

"I really did think he would choose me," she said, softly.

And when Angelina looked up again, Petronella had gone.

Dorothea was far less gracious. If she was worried about her younger sister, the only way she showed it was in an officious need to micromanage the trousseau that Benedetto was funding for his new bride along with everything else.

"If he's a murderer," Angelina had said tightly one afternoon, after Dorothea made her try on armful after armful of concoctions she'd ordered straight from atelier in Paris on Angelina's behalf, "do you really think that choosing the right selection of negligees will save me?"

"Don't be ridiculous," Dorothea tutted, bustling about Angelina's bedchamber as if she'd never sat on a settee wailing about her impending death. "You know how people like to talk. That's all it is, I'm certain. A series of tragic events and too many rumors and innuendos."

"I hope you're right," Angelina had said.

But Dorothea's only response had been to lay out more soft, frilly things for Angelina to try on.

And it was a strange thing indeed to know that her life had changed completely—to understand that nothing she knew would be hers any longer, and soon—when for thirty days, only the trappings of her life changed. The manor house slowly returned to its former glory. Her father laughed again. Margrete looked less stiff and tense around the eyes.

But Angelina still woke in her same old

bed. She still timed her breakfast to avoid the rest of the family, and then set off for her long morning walk, no matter the weather. She still played the piano for hours, alone in the conservatory.

If it weren't for the endless hammering, she might have been tempted to imagine that she'd made the whole thing up.

Then again, every time that Benedetto visited—a stolen evening here, a day or two there—the balance in Angelina's family… shifted.

Because she was shifting, she thought as she lay in her bed at night with her hands between her legs, not sure if she wanted to sob or scream out all the wildfires he'd lit inside her. With that dark gaze. With the things he did to her when they were alone. His mouth, his fingers. And always that dark, seductive laugh.

She had always thought of a seduction as something…quicker. The mistake of an evening. Something hasty and ill-considered that would take time and space to repent.

But Benedetto taught her many lessons about time. And patience.

And the exquisite torture of anticipation.

The only thing Angelina had ever wanted was her piano and a place to play it. She had been certain she knew herself inside and out. But this man taught her—over and over—that there were banked fires in her she hardly understood.

Dark, greedy claws that dug in, deep, whenever he touched her and when he did not. Red and terrible longings that made her toss and turn when she wanted to sleep.

This hunger that made her run to him when she knew full well she should have run the other way.

"Such a pretty, needy little thing you are," he murmured one evening.

Like all the nights he came here, there had first been the awkward family dinner where he'd demonstrated his mastery over her father, then cowed her sisters and mother into uncharacteristic silence—usually with little more than a lift of one dangerous brow. When her mother and sisters repaired to the drawing room, leaving her father to his solitary port, Benedetto would usher Angelina to the conservatory.

It was the same every time.

That long, *fraught* walk through a house only half-alive. The sound of his footsteps mingled with hers. The humming, overfull silence stretched out between them and echoing back from the walls. Her breath would change as they moved, and she was certain he could hear it, though he always remained behind her. And he never spoke.

She told herself she marched toward her own, slow execution. She walked herself off the plank.

But the truth she never wished to face was that the closer they got to the conservatory, the quicker her steps. The quicker her breath.

And oh, how molten and hot her blood ran in her, pooling between her legs with a desperate intent.

Because inside that room, who knew what might happen?

He always made her play.

And then he played her, always making

her scream and arch and shake. Always his wicked fingers, his clever mouth, tasting her, tempting her.

Training her, something in her whispered.

"Is this how you murder them all?" she asked one evening, a scant week away from their wedding.

Benedetto had laid her out on the chaise that had appeared one morning, along with all kinds of furniture throughout the *château*. It was as if the house was a visual representation of her own femininity, and she could see it grow its own pleasure. Lush and deep.

Paintings reappeared. Priceless antiques took their places once again. There were updates everywhere, light where there had been darkness, the cobwebs swept away and cracks plastered over.

She'd forgotten herself, with her skirts tossed up and his head so dark between her thighs.

She'd forgotten herself, but she remembered with a jolt when she shifted and caught a glimpse of them in the fogged-up windows that surrounded them on all sides.

Benedetto was so big, tall and strong, and she was laid out before him, splayed wide like an offering. He was eating her alive and she was letting him, but she should never have let herself forget that the pleasure he visited upon her untried body was a weapon.

Everything about this man was a weapon only he knew how to use.

"I didn't mean that," she managed to gasp out while her heart galloped inside her, lust and fear and that same dark ache fusing into one.

She tried to pull her legs closed but his broad shoulders were between them, and he did not move. He lifted his head and his night-black eyes bored into her. He pressed his palm, roughened and huge, against the faint swell of her abdomen.

And something about the pressure made a new, dangerous heat uncurl inside her.

"What do you know of marriage?" he asked, and his voice was as dark as the rest of him, insinuating and dangerous.

She could feel that prickle that was as much

longing as it was fear sweep over her body, leaving goose bumps in its wake.

"I have never been married before."

Angelina didn't know why she was answering him so prosaically. When she was as he liked her, still dressed for dinner but with her skirts around her waist, so she was bared only to him. Bared and wet and aching again.

Sometimes she thought the aching might actually kill her, here in this house before she had the chance to leave it, and that notion made her want to sob out loud.

Other times, she hoped it would.

Benedetto shifted his weight so that he held himself up on one crooked elbow. He let his hand drift from her abdomen to her secret, greedy flesh.

"Put your hands above your head," he told her, and she knew it was an order. A command she should have ignored while she still could, but her arms were already moving of their own accord. Lifting over her head so that her back arched and her breasts pressed wantonly against the bodice of the old dress she wore.

She knew he liked that. She knew a lot of the things he liked, by now. He liked her hair free and unconfined, tangled about wherever he lay her. He liked to get his fingers in it so he could guide her head where he wanted it. Particularly when he kissed her, tongue and teeth and a sheer mastery that made her shiver.

"Tell me what you know of men, Angelina," he said now, stroking the bright need between her legs, though he had already had her sweating, shaking, crying out his name.

This time, when her hips began to move, he found her opening. And he began to work one of those blunt, surprisingly tough fingers into her depths of her body.

She felt the stretching. The ache in her intensified.

Her nipples were delirious points, and every time she breathed, the way her breasts jarred against the fabric of her bra made her want to jerk away. Or move closer.

"I have never spent much time with men," she managed to pant out. "I had a piano tutor, a boy from the village, but I learned all he had to teach me long ago."

"Did you play for him as you play for me?" Benedetto asked, his voice something like a croon—but much, much darker. "Did you open your legs like this? Did you let him slip between your thighs and taste your heat?"

And even as he asked those questions, he added a second finger to the first. He began to stroke his way deep inside her, and the sensation made it impossible to think. Impossible to do anything but lift her hips to meet him, then try to get away, or both at once.

His hand found a rhythm, but her hips took convincing.

"N-No..." She wasn't sure what, precisely, she was saying *no* to. His fingers plunged, withdrew. Then again. And again. A driving, relentless taking. "No one has ever touched me."

"Not even you?" he asked. "Late at night, tucked up beneath your covers in this tomb of a house? Do you not reach down, slip your fingers into all this molten greed, and make yourself shudder into life?"

Angelina was bright red already. But the flash of heat that he kindled within her swept over her until she was making a keening, high-pitched cry. Her hips finally found their rhythm, thrusting against him wildly as her head fell back.

And she thrashed there, not sure how anyone could survive these little deaths, much less the bigger one that waited for her.

Not sure anyone should.

"Look at me," Benedetto ordered her.

She realized she didn't know how much time had passed. How long she had shaken like that, open and exposed. It took her a long while to crack open her eyes. She struggled to sit up because he was sitting too, regarding her in his typically sinful and wicked way.

Angelina couldn't tell if it was shame or desire that worked inside of her, then.

Especially when he held her gaze, lifted the fingers he'd had inside her, and slowly licked them clean.

She heard herself gasping for breath as if she was running. If she was running to escape him, the way she knew she should. She could crash through the windows into the gardens that her parents had let go to seed, and were now manicured and pruned. She could race into the summer night, leaving all this behind her.

She could save herself and let her family do as they would.

But she only gazed back at him, breathing too heavily, and did not move an inch to extricate from this man who held her tight in his grip—though he was not touching her at all.

"I want you desperate, always," he told her, his voice that same, serious command. "I want you wet and needy, Angelina. When I look at you, I want to know that while you look like an angel, here, where you are naked and only ever mine, you are nothing but heat and hunger."

"Do you mean...?"

"I mean you should touch yourself. Taste yourself, if you wish. I insist. As long as you are always ready for me."

She understood what he meant by *ready* in a different way, now. Because it was one thing to read about sex. To read about that strange, inevitable joining. She understood the mechanics, but was not until now, so close to her wedding night, that she understood that it would be far more than merely *mechanical.*

Benedetto's head tilted slightly to one side. "Do you understand me?"

"I do," she said, and his smile was dark.

"Then I do not think, little one, that you need to worry overmuch about murder."

That was the last time she'd seen him.

She pushed herself upright in her bed this morning, her head as fuzzy as if she'd helped herself to the liquor in the drawing room when she didn't dare. Not when she had Benedetto to contend with and needed all her wits about her.

And it shocked her, as she looked around her room, that there was a lump in her throat as she accepted the reality that this room would no longer be hers by the time the sun set.

Her bedchamber had already undergone renovations, like so much of the house had in the past month. It already looked like some-one else's. Plush, quietly elegant rugs were strewn about the floors, taking the chill away. She'd forgotten entirely that once, long ago, there had been curtains and drapes and a canopy over her bed, but they were all back now.

He'd given her back her childhood so she would know exactly what she was leaving behind her when she left here today.

She got up and headed to her bathroom, walking gingerly because she could feel the neediest, greediest part of her ripe and ready—just the way he wanted her. But she paused in the doorway. Because she could no longer hear the symphony of the old pipes.

And when she turned on the water in her sink, it ran hot.

Angelina ran herself a bath and climbed in, running her hands over her slick, soapy skin. Her breasts felt larger. Her belly was so sensitive she sucked in a breath through her teeth when she touched it.

And when she ran her hands between her legs, to do as he'd commanded her, she was hotter than the water around her.

Then hotter still as she imagined his face,

dark and knowing, and made the water splash over the sides of her tub onto the floor.

But too soon, then it was time to dress.

Margrete bustled in, her sisters in her wake like sulky attendants. And for a long while, the three of them worked in silence. Petronella piled Angelina's hair on top of her head and pinned in sparkling hints of stones that looked like diamonds. Dorothea fussed with her dress, fastening each of the parade of buttons that marched down her spine. Margrete called in Matrice, the notably less surly housemaid now that there was money, and the two of them packed Angelina's things.

Petronella did Angelina's makeup. She made her younger sister's face almost otherworldly, and did something with her battery of brushes and sponges that made Angelina's eyes seemed bluer than the summer sky.

Matrice left first, wheeling out Angelina's paltry belongings with her.

And there was no need to keep her hiding place a secret now, so Angelina let her mother and sisters watch as she walked over to the four posts of her bed, unscrewed one tall taper, and pulled out her grandmother's pearls.

Her sisters passed a dark look between them while Angelina fastened the dark, moody pearls around her neck and let the weight of them settle there, against her collarbone.

And then her mother led her to the cheval glass.

The dress had arrived without warning two weeks before the wedding. Angelina had tried it on and let the seamstress who'd arrived with it take her measurements and make her alterations. The dress had seemed simple. Pretty. Not too much, somehow.

But now there was no escaping the dress or what it meant or what would become of her. She stared into the mirror, and a bride stared back.

The dark pearls she'd looped around her neck looked like a bruise, but everything else was white. Flowing, frothy white, while her hair seemed silvery and gleaming and impossible on top of her head.

She looked like what she was.

A virgin sacrifice to a dark king.

"You must ask him for what you want," Margrete told her, her voice matter-of-fact, but her eyes dark. "A piano, for example."

"He has already promised me a Steinway."

Margrete moved the skirt of the wedding gown this way, then that. "You must not be afraid to make demands, but you must also submit to his." Again, a touch of her dark gaze in the mirror. "No matter what, Angelina. Do you understand me? With a smile, if possible."

Angelina expected her sisters to chime in then, making arch comments about sex and their experiences, but they were silent. She looked in the glass and found them sitting on the end of her bed, looking…she would have said lost, if they had been anyone else.

"I'm not afraid of his demands," she said.

It wasn't until her mother's gaze snapped to hers again that she realized perhaps she ought to have been.

"You must remember that no matter what, you need only call and I will come to you," Margrete said then, as if she was making her own vows.

Angelina could not have been more shocked if her mother had shared sordid details of her own sexual exploits. "I… Really?"

Margrete turned Angelina then, taking her by the shoulders so she could look into her face.

"You're not the first girl to be ransomed off for the benefit of her family," Margrete said in a low, direct voice. "My father lost me in a card game."

There was a muffled sound of surprise from the bed. But their mother did not wait for that astonishing remark to sink in. Margrete lifted her chin, her fingers gripping Angelina's shoulders so hard she was half worried they would leave a mark.

"Life is what you make of it. Some parts are unpleasant, others regretful—but those are things you cannot control. You can always control yourself. You can school your reactions. You can master your own heart. And no one can ever take that from you, Angelina. No one."

"But Papa…" Angelina was turning over

the idea of a card game and her severe grandfather in her head. "Papa was not a murderer."

"All men are murderers." Margrete's dark eyes flashed. "They take a daughter and make her a woman whether she wants it or not. They kill a girl to create a wife, then a mother. It's all a question of degrees, child."

And with those words, Margrete took her youngest daughter by the hand and led her down the grand, restored stair to the ballroom, where she handed Angelina off to her father.

The father who had *won* her mother, not wooed her, as Angelina had always found so hard to imagine.

The father who did not look at the daughter he was sacrificing to line his pockets even once as he marched her down the aisle, then married her off to a monster.

CHAPTER FIVE

BENEDETTO TOLERATED THE CEREMONY.

Barely.

God knew, he was tired of weddings.

His angel walked toward him, spurred on to unseemly haste by her portly father, who was practically salivating at the opportunity to hand her over to Benedetto's keeping. Or to her death. That Anthony Charteris had not required Benedetto to make any statements or promises about Angelina's well-being showed exactly what kind of man he was.

Tiny. Puny. Greedy and selfish to his core.

But then, Benedetto already knew that. If Anthony hadn't been precisely that kind of man, he wouldn't have come to Benedetto's notice.

As weddings went, this one was painless enough. There was no spectacle, no grand cathedral, no pageant. The words were said, and quickly, and the only ones he cared about came from Angelina's mouth.

"I do," she said, her voice quiet, but not weak. "I will."

He slid a ring onto her hand and felt his own greed kick hard enough inside that he could hardly set himself apart from Charteris. What moral high ground did he think *he* inhabited?

Soon, he told himself. *Soon enough.*

The priest intoned the words that bound them, and then it was done.

He was married for the seventh time. The last time, he dared to hope, though there was no reason to imagine he could make it so.

There was no reason to imagine this would be anything but the same old grind. The lies, the distrust. In his head he saw a key in a lock, and a bare white room with nothing but the sea outside it.

Oh, yes. He knew how this would end.

But despite everything, something in him wished it could be otherwise. Her music sang in him, and though he knew better, it felt like hope.

Once the ceremony was over and Angelina was his wife, he saw no reason to subject himself to Charteris or his family any longer. With any luck, neither he nor Angelina would ever see any of them again—for one reason or another.

He left Angelina to the tender mercies of her mother and sisters for the last time. He cut through the small gathering, ignoring the guests that Charteris had invited purely to boast about his sudden reversal of fortune, something that was easy to do when they all shrank from him in fear. And when he reached the place where Anthony was holding court, he scared off the cluster around him with a single freezing stare.

"My man of business will contact you," he told his seventh father-in-law with as little inflection as possible. "He will be your point person from now on for anything involving the house or the settlement I've arranged. Personal communications from you will not be necessary. And will no longer be accepted."

"Yes, yes," Charteris brayed pompously, already florid of cheek and glassy of eye, which told Benedetto all he needed to know about how this man had lost the fortune he'd been born with and the one he'd married into, as well. "I was thinking we might well have a ball—"

"You may have whatever you wish," Benedetto said with a soft menace that might as well have been a growl. "You may throw a ball every weekend. You may build a *château* in every corner of France, for all I care. The money is yours to do with as you wish. But what you will not have is any familiarity with me. Or any access to your daughter without my permission. Do you understand?"

He could see the older man process the rebuke like the slap it was, and then, just as quickly, understand that it would not affect his wallet. He did not actually shrug. But it was implied.

"I wish you and my daughter every happiness," Charteris replied.

He raised his glass. Benedetto inclined his head, disgusted.

And then he went to retrieve his seventh wife.

As he drew closer to the little knot she stood in with her mother and sisters, he felt something pierce his chest at the sight of her. Gleaming. Angelic.

All that, and the way she played the piano made him hard.

And that was nothing next to her taste.

Something in him growled like the sort of monster he tried so hard to keep hidden in public. Because people so readily saw all kinds of fiends when they looked at him—why should he confirm their worst suspicions?

"Come," he said, when his very appearance set them all to wide-eyed silence. "It is time to take you to my castle, wife."

He watched the ripple of that sentence move through the four of them. He could see the words *Butcher of Castello Nero* hanging in the air around them.

And whatever he thought of Anthony Charteris, whatever impressions he'd gleaned of these women over the past month, they all paled in unison now.

Because everyone knew, after all, what happened to a Franceschi bride. Everyone knew the fate that awaited her.

For the first time, the things others thought about him actually…got to him.

Benedetto held out his hand.

The Charteris sisters remained white-faced. Their mother was made of stouter stuff, however, and the look she fixed on him might have been loathing, for all the good it would do her.

But it was Angelina who mattered. Angelina whose cheeks did not pale, but flushed instead with a brighter color he knew well by now.

Angelina, his seventh bride, who murmured something soothing in the direction of her mother and sisters and then slid her delicate hand into his.

Then she let him lead her from her father's house, never to return.

Not if he had anything to say about it.

He assisted her into the back of the gleaming black car that waited for them, joining her in the back seat. He lounged there, as the voluminous skirts of her soft white wedding gown flowed in every direction, like seafoam.

Benedetto found he liked thinking of her that way, like a mermaid rising from the deep. A creature of story and fable.

"Why have you waited to…seal our bargain until our wedding night?" she asked as the car pulled away from the front of the old house that was already starting to look like itself again. Its old glory restored for the small price of Angelina's life.

What a bargain, he thought darkly.

Of course, neither Angelina nor her noxious father had any idea of the bargain he intended to pose to her directly—but he was getting ahead of himself.

And if this time was different—if he had found himself captivated by this woman in ways he did not fully understand and had never experienced before—well. He was sure he would pay a great penance for that, too, before long.

But she was gazing at him, waiting for him to answer her.

"It is customary to wait, is it not?" Because he was happy to have her think him deeply traditional. For now. He watched her, but she did not turn around to watch her life disappear behind her. So she did not see her sisters, clutching each other's hands as they stood at the top of the stairs, staring after her. She did not see her mother in the window, her face twisting. She did not note the absence of her father from these scenes of despair. "Some things have fallen out of favor in these dark times, I have no doubt, but I hope a white wedding will always be in fashion." He allowed his mouth to curve. "Or a slightly off-white wedding, in this case. It is your piano playing, I fear. It undoes all my good intentions."

Angelina looked at him, her blue eyes searching his face though her own looked hot. "You have had many lovers, if the tabloids are to be believed."

"First, you must never believe the tabloids. They are paid to write fiction, not fact. But second, I have always kept my affairs and my wives separate."

She cleared her throat. "And now? Will you continue in the same vein?"

He picked up her hand, and toyed with the ring he'd put there, that great, gleaming red ruby that shone like blood in the summer light that fell in through the car windows. "What is it you are asking me?"

"Do you conduct your affairs while you're married?" She sat straighter, though she didn't snatch her hand back from him. "Will one of my duties be to look the other way?"

"Are you asking me if I plan to be faithful? Less than an hour after we said our vows before God, man, and your father's creditors?"

"I am. Do you?"

Again, he was struck by how different she was from the rest of his brides—none of whom had seemed to care who he touched, or when. It was as if Angelina had cast a spell on him. Enchanted him, despite everything.

"As faithful as you are to me, Angelina."

His voice was darker than it should have been, but it was one more thing he couldn't seem to control around her. "That is how faithful I will be to you in return."

This time he was certain he could see those words, like another set of vows, fill up the car like the voluminous skirts she wore.

"That's easy enough then," she replied with that tartness that surprised and delighted him every time she dared show it. "I have only ever loved one thing in my life. My piano. As long as you provide me with one to play as I wish, as you promised, why shouldn't I keep the promises I made to you?"

He lifted her hand to his mouth, and then, idly, sucked one of her fingers into the heat of his mouth.

"I've never understood cheating," she continued, her voice prim, though he could see the way she trembled. He could taste it. "Surely it cannot be that difficult to keep a vow. And if it is, why make it in the first place?"

"Ah, yes. The certainty of youth." He applied more suction, and she shuddered beautifully. "You know very little of passion, I think. It has a habit of making a mockery of those who think in terms of black and white."

Her eyes were much too blue. "Have you cheated on your wives before?"

And he had expected silence. That was typical. Or if there were questions, this being Angelina who seemed so shockingly unafraid of him, perhaps more pointed questions about murderers or mysterious deaths. Or euphemisms that didn't quite mention either. But not this. Not what he was tempted to imagine was actual possessiveness on her part. He noted that the hand he was not holding was balled into a fist.

Benedetto would have sworn that he was far too jaded for passion to make a mockery of him, and yet here he was. Hoping for things that could never be.

"I have never had the opportunity to grow bored," he replied, deliberately. With no little edge to his voice. "They were all gone too soon."

He watched her swallow hard. He watched the column of her neck move.

He wished he could watch himself and this dance of his as closely.

"You have not told me your expectations," she said, shifting her gaze away from him and aiming it somewhere in front of her. He found he missed the weight of her regard. "You're obviously a very wealthy man. Many wealthy men have staff to take on the position normally held by a wife."

"I assure you that I do not intend to take my staff to my bed."

He saw the lovely red color on her cheeks brighten further but she pushed on, and her carefully even voice did not change. "I'm not referring to your bed. I'm referring to the duties involved in running a great house. Or in your case, a castle."

"You are welcome to engage my housekeeper in battle for supremacy, Angelina. But I warn you, Signora Malandra is a fearsome creature indeed. And jealously guards what she sees as hers."

His bride looked at him then, narrowly. "Does that include you?"

Benedetto shrugged, keeping his face impassive though he was once again pleased with her possessiveness. "She's been with my family for a very long time. You could argue that in many ways, she raised me. So yes, I suppose she does see me as hers. But she is not my lover, if that is what you are asking."

He didn't actually laugh at that. Or the very notion of suggesting such a thing where his housekeeper could hear it.

Angelina managed to give the impression of bristling without actually doing so. "It had not occurred to me that you might install your lovers under the same roof as your wife. Though perhaps, given your infamy, I should anticipate such things."

"I will not do anything of the kind," he drawled, trying to sound lazy enough that the car would not reverberate with the truth in his words. "But whether you believe that or not will be up to you."

"You expect me to be jealous?"

"I'm not afraid of jealousy, Angelina. On the contrary. I do not understand why it is considered a virtue to pretend the heart is not a greedy organ when we can all feel it pump and clench in our chests. Lust starts there. And where there is lust, where there is need and want and longing, there will always be jealousy." He shrugged. "This is the curse of humanity, no? It is better to embrace the darkness than to pretend it does not or cannot exist."

"Jealousy is destructive," she said, again in that matter-of-fact tone he suspected was a product of her youth.

"That depends what you are building," he replied. "And whether or not you find beauty in the breaking of it."

And then he laughed, darkly and too knowingly, as she reddened yet again.

It was not a long drive to the private airfield where his plane waited for them. Once there, he escorted her up the stairs and then into the jet's luxurious cabin.

Angelina looked around at the ostentatious display of his wealth and power and swallowed, hard. "Are my things here? I can change—"

"I think not," he said, with a quiet relish.

"You will remain in that gown until I remove it myself, little one."

Again, that glorious flush that made her glow. Her lips fell open while her pulse went wild in her throat. "But… But how long…?"

"We will have a wedding night," he assured her, though wedding nights with him were rarely what his brides imagined. "Were you worried?"

"Of course not," she said.

But she was lying. He could hear the music she played in his head. He could remember all too well those steamy evenings in that barren room that she'd filled with art and longing and her own sweet cries of need and release.

He was entirely too tempted to indulge himself—because he couldn't recall the last time he'd been tempted at all.

Benedetto tilted his head slightly as he regarded her, not surprised when that bright glow crept down her neck. "You have my permission to please yourself as you wish if you find you cannot wait. No need to lock yourself away." He indicated one of the plush leather seats in the cabin. "Pull up your skirts, bare yourself to me, and show me your pleasure, Angelina."

He could hear her ragged breath as she took that in. "I… I can't."

Her voice was barely a whisper.

"Then you must suffer, wife. And you must wait."

And he watched her almost idly as he handled matters of business on the short flight. She sat in her seat as if it was made of nails, shifting this way, and that. Clearly squirming with anticipation, though he supposed she might lie to them both about that. Too bad it was stamped all over her.

He couldn't wait to indulge himself. He, who usually preferred his wedding nights be more theater than anything else.

Why couldn't he stick to the script with this woman?

They landed in Italy on another private airfield not far from the coast where the Franceschis had lived for centuries. He ushered her into another car that waited for them, gleaming in the afternoon sun, but this time he drove it himself.

"We must hurry if we wish to make the tide," he told her.

And the dress she wore barely fit into the bucket seats of the low-slung sports car. But the helpless, needy sound he heard her make when he put the car into gear could only be a harbinger of things to come.

If he let it.

And oh, how he wanted to let it. He had already tasted her—and he couldn't seem to get past that. He couldn't seem to keep his head together when he was near her. He couldn't remember his duties, and that spelled disaster.

He knew all that, and still, all he could focus on was her reaction to his car.

He could imagine the way the low, throaty growl of the engine worked its way through her where she sat. But even if he couldn't, the way she began to breathe—too heavily—told him what he needed to know.

She might not like him. She might want him for the concert piano he'd had made especially for her. She might choose to leave him like all the rest, and soon.

But she wanted him.

Desperately.

There was an honesty in that. And it was new. Completely different from the six who'd come before her.

Benedetto found he was less interested in her sensual suffering than he probably should have been.

"I cannot wait, Angelina," he told her now. "I want you to lift your wedding gown to your waist, as if we were back in your stark conservatory."

And he could tell the state she was in when she didn't argue. Or stammer. Or even blush again.

He shifted the car into second gear as he raced down the old roads toward the coastline his grandparents had kept undeveloped, even when that had required they fight off "progress" with their own hands, and watched as she obeyed him.

So quickly her hands were shaking.

"Good girl," he murmured when she'd bared all the soft, silken flesh of her thighs to his gaze. He could only glance at all that warm lushness as he drove, faster and faster, but it was enough. It made him so hard he ached with it. "Touch yourself. I want you to do whatever you need to do to come, Angelina. Fast and hard. Now."

She let out a sound that could have been a sob. A moan.

But he knew when she'd found her own heat, because she made a sound that was as full of relief as it was greed.

It made his sex pulse.

And he drove too fast down the coastal road he knew by heart. Then he sped up as he hit the treacherous drive that stretched out into the water that rose higher and higher by the moment as the tide came in and began to swallow it whole.

"Come," he ordered her.

She rocked her hips, making mindless, glorious little sounds. He could hear the greediness of her flesh, and a quick glance beside him found her with her head thrown back and her hands buried between her legs. The summer afternoon light streamed into the sports car, bouncing off the water and making her so bright, she nearly burned.

So beautiful, it cut at him.

So perfectly innocent, it should have shamed him, but it didn't. Not when he wanted her this much.

If he hadn't been a monster already, this would have made him one, he was sure of it.

Benedetto heard her breath catch. Her head rocked back, and he was sure that he could feel her heat as if it was his hands on her, clutched deep in her molten core. That hot rush of sweet, wet fire as she took herself over the edge.

She shook and she sobbed, and he drove faster. There was light and water and his seventh bride, coming on command. And when her sobs had settled into a harsh panting, he reached over. He took one of her hands, and sucked her fingers into his mouth because that heat was all for him. It was his.

She was his, and no matter if that damned them both, he didn't have it in him to stop this madness. He couldn't.

"Open your eyes, Angelina," he told her then, another soft order. "We are here."

That was how he drove her into Castello Nero, the ancestral home of his cursed and terrible clan. Flushed and wanton, wet and greedy, the taste of her in his mouth and that wild, ravaged look on her face.

Welcome home, little one, Benedetto thought darkly.

And then he delivered them both into their doom.

CHAPTER SIX

ANGELINA BARELY HAD the presence of mind to shove her skirts back down, letting the yards and yards of soft white fabric flow back into place. To preserve whatever was left of her modesty.

Though she almost laughed at the thought of modesty after…that. After the past month, after this drive—what was left for him to take?

But, of course, she knew the answer to that.

And imagining what she had to lose here in this place made it difficult to breathe.

The castle keep rose on all sides, the stone gleaming in the summer afternoon light. The sunshine made it seem magical instead of malevolent, and she tried her best to cling to that impression.

But her body felt like his, not hers. Even

her breath seemed to saw in and out of her in an alien rhythm.

His, she thought again. Not hers.

Benedetto swung out of the car but Angelina stayed where she was. The drive from the airfield had been a blur of heat, need, and the endless explosion that was still reverberating through her bones, her flesh. Still, she could picture the car eating up the narrow road that flirted with the edge of the incoming tide on what was little more than a raised sandbar. Some of the waves had already been tipping over the edge of the bar to sneak across the road as Benedetto had floored his engine. It was only a matter of time before water covered the causeway completely.

And all the molten heat in the world, all of which was surely pooled between her legs even now, couldn't keep her from recognizing the salient point here in a very different way than she had when she was merely thinking about Castello Nero instead of experiencing it herself.

Which was that once the tide rose, she

would be stuck here on the island that was his castle.

Stranded here, in fact.

"How long is it between tides?" she had asked at the family dinner table one night while Benedetto was there, oozing superiority and brooding masculinity from where he lounged there at the foot of the table, his hot gaze on her.

Because she might have already betrayed herself where this man was concerned, but that didn't mean she hadn't read up on him.

"Six hours," Dorothea had said stoutly.

"Or a lifetime," Benedetto had replied, sounding darkly entertained.

She could feel her heart race again, the way it had when she'd been back in the relative safety of her father's house. But it was much different here, surrounded by the stone walls and ramparts. Now that this was where she was expected to stay. High tide or low.

Come what may.

The door beside her opened, and he was there. Her forbiddingly beautiful husband, who was looking down at her with his mouth slightly curved in one corner and that knowing look in his too-dark eyes.

And his hand was no less rough or insinuating when he helped her from the sports car. No matter where he touched her, it seemed, she shuddered.

“Welcome home, wife,” he said.

The ancient castle loomed behind him, a gleaming stone facade that seemed to throb with portent and foreboding. It had been built to be a fortress. But to Angelina’s mind, that only meant it could make a good prison.

The summer sky was deceptively bright up above. The castle’s many towers and turrets would surely have punctured any clouds that happened by. Her heart still beat at her, a rushing, rhythm—

But in the next moment, Angelina understood that what she was hearing was the sea. The lap of tide against the rocks and the stone walls.

She didn’t know if that odd giddiness she felt then was terror or relief.

When she looked back at her husband, that same devil that had worked in her the first night he'd come to her father's house brushed itself off. And sat up.

"Why do you call me 'wife' instead of my name?" she asked.

"Did you not marry me?" he asked lazily, giving the impression of lounging about when he was standing there before her, his hands thrust into the pockets of the dark bespoke suit he wore that made him look urbane and untamed at once. "Are you not my wife?"

"I rather thought it was because all the names run together," Angelina said dryly. "There have been so many."

She didn't know what possessed her to say such a thing to the man who had rendered Margrete Charteris silent. Or how she dared.

But to her surprise, he laughed.

It was a rich, sensuous sound she knew too well from back in her father's conservatory. Here, it seemed to echo back from the ancient stone walls, then wrapped as tightly around her as the bodice of the wedding dress she wore.

"I never forget a name." He inclined his head to her. "Angelina."

Hearing her name in his mouth made the echo of his dark laughter inside her seem to hum.

Benedetto took his time shifting his gaze from her then. He focused on something behind her, then nodded.

That was when Angelina realized they were not, as she'd imagined, alone out here in this medieval keep. She turned, her neck suddenly prickling, and saw an older woman standing there, dressed entirely in black as if in perpetual mourning. The housekeeper, if she had to guess, with a long, drawn face and a sharp, unfriendly gaze.

"This is your new mistress," Benedetto told the woman, who only sniffed. "Angelina, may I present Signora Malandra, keeper of my castle."

"Enchanté," the older woman said in crisp, cut-glass French that did not match her Italian name.

"I'm so pleased to make your acquaintance," Angelina murmured, and even smiled prettily, because Signora Malandra might have been off-putting, but she was no match for Margrete Charteris.

"Come," said Angelina's brand-new husband, once again fixing that dark gaze of his on her. "I will show you to the bedchamber."

The bedchamber, Angelina noted. Not *her* bedchamber.

Her heart, having only just calmed itself, kicked into high gear again.

He did not release her hand. He pulled her with him as he moved, towing her through an archway cut into the heavy stone wall. Then he drew her into the interior of one of the oldest castles in Italy.

She still felt off balance from what had happened in his car, but she tried to take note of her surroundings. *Should you have to run for your life,* something dark inside her whispered. She tried her best to shove it aside—at least while she was in her husband's presence.

Unlike the house where she'd grown up, Castello Nero was flush with wealth and luxury. Benedetto took her down corridors filled with marble, from the floors to the statues in the carved alcoves, to benches set here and there as if the expectation was that one might need to rest while taking in all the art and magnificence.

He laughed at her expression. “Did you expect a crumbling Gothic ruin?”

She blinked, disquieted at the notion he could read her so easily. “I keep imagining kings and queens around every tapestry, that’s all.”

“My family have held many titles over time,” he told her as they walked. Down long hallways that must have stretched the length of the tidal island. “A count here, a duke there, but nobility is much like the tide, is it not? In favor one century, forbidden the next.”

Angelina’s family considered itself old money rather than new, but they did not speak in terms of *centuries.* They were still focused on a smattering of generations. The difference struck her as staggering, suddenly.

“The castle has remained in the family no matter the revolutions, exiles, or abdications that have plagued Europe,” Benedetto said. “Titles were stripped, ancestors were beheaded, but in one form or another this island has been in my family since the fall of the Roman Empire. Or thereabouts."

Angelina tried to imagine what it must feel like to be personally connected to the long march of so much history—and to have a family castle to mark the passage of all that time.

"Did you grow up here?" she asked.

Because it was impossible to imagine. She couldn't conceive of children running around in this shining museum, laughing or shrieking in the silent halls. And more, she couldn't picture Benedetto ever having been a child himself. Much less engaging in anything like an ungainly adolescence. And certainly not here, in a swirl of ancient armor and sumptuous tapestries, depicting historical scenes that as far as Angelina knew, might have been the medieval version of photo albums and scrapbooks.

"In a sense," he replied.

He had led her into a gallery, the sort she recognized all too well. It was covered with formal, painted portraits, she didn't have to lean in to read the embossed nameplates to understand that she was looking at centuries of his ancestors. The sweep of history as represented by various Franceschis across time. From monks to noblemen to what looked entirely too much like a vampire in one dark painting.

Benedetto gazed at the pictures on the wall, not at her. “My parents preferred their own company and my grandfather thought children were useless until properly educated. When my parents died my grandfather—and Signora Malandra—were forced to take over what parenting was required at that point. I was a teenager then and luckily for us all, I was usually at boarding school. It felt like home. I was first sent there at five.”

Angelina had never given a single thought to the parenting choices she might make one day, yet she knew, somehow, that she did not have it in her to send such a tiny child away like that. Off to the tender mercies of strangers. Something in her chilled at the thought.

“Did you like boarding school?” she asked.

Benedetto stopped before a portrait that she

guessed, based on the more modern clothing alone, might have been his parents. She studied the picture as if she was looking for clues. The woman had dark glossy hair and a heart-stoppingly beautiful face. She sat demurely in a grand chair, dressed in a gown of royal blue. Behind her chair stood a man who looked remarkably like Benedetto, though he had wings of white in his dark hair. And if possible, his mouth looked crueler. His nose more like a Roman coin.

"There was no question of liking it or not liking it," Benedetto said, gazing at the portrait. Then he turned that gaze on her, and she found the way his eyes glittered made her chest feel constricted. "It was simply the reality of my youth. My mother always felt that her duties were in the providing of the heir. Never in the raising of him."

"And did… Did your parents…?"

Angelina didn't even know what she was asking. She'd done what due diligence she could over the past month. Meaning she had Googled her husband-to-be and his family to see what she could find. Mostly, as this castle seemed to advertise, it seemed the Franceschi family was renowned for wealth and periodic cruelty stretching back to the dawn of time. In that, however, she had to admit that they were no different from any other storied European family. It was only Benedetto—in modern times, at any rate—who had a reputation worse than that of any other pedigreed aristocrat.

His mother had been considered one of the most beautiful women in the world. She and Benedetto's father had run in a glittering, hard-edged crowd, chasing and throwing parties in the gleaming waters of the Côte d'Azur or the non-touristy parts of the Caribbean. Or in sprawling villas in places like Amalfi, Manhattan, or wherever else the sparkling people were.

"Did my parents regret their choices in some way?" Benedetto laughed, as if the very idea was a great joke. "How refreshingly earnest. The only thing my parents ever agreed upon was a necessity of securing the Franceschi line. Once I was born, their duties were discharged and they happily returned to the things they did best. My father preferred pain to pleasure. And as my mother was a martyr, if only to causes that suited her self-importance, they were in many ways a match made in heaven."

Angelina's mouth was too dry. "P-Pain to pleasure?"

Benedetto's eyes gleamed. "He was a celebrated sadist. And not only in the bedroom."

Angelina didn't know what expression she must have had on her face, but it made Benedetto laugh again. Then he drew her behind him once more, leading her out of this gallery filled with black Franceschi eyes and dark secrets, and deeper into the castle.

"Why is that something you know about your own father?" she managed to ask, fighting to keep her voice from whispering off into nothingness. "Surely a son should be protected from such knowledge."

Benedetto's laugh, then, was more implied than actual. But Angelina could feel it shiver through her all the same.

"Even if my parents had exhibited a modicum of modesty, which they did not, the pa-

parazzi were only too happy to fill in the details before and after their deaths. Barring that, I can't tell you the number of times one or other of their friends—and by friends, I mean rivals, enemies, former lovers, and compatriots—thought they might as well sidle up to me with some ball or other and share. In excruciating detail." He glanced down at her, his mouth curved. "They are little better than jackals, these highborn creatures who spend their lives throwing fortunes down this or that drain. Every last one of them."

"Including you?" She dared to ask.

That curve in the corner of his mouth took on a bitter cast. "Especially me."

Together they climbed a series of stairs until they finally made it to a hall made of windows. Modern windows in place of a wall on one side, all of them looking out over the sea. Angelina could see that the wind had picked up, capping the waves in white, which should have added to the anxiety frothing inside her. Instead, the sight soothed her.

The sea carried on, no matter what happened within these walls.

It made her imagine that she might, too.

Despite everything she knew to the contrary.

"This is the private wing of the castle," Benedetto told her as they walked beside the windows. "The nursery is at one end and the master suite far on the other end, behind many walls and doors, so the master of the house need never disturb his sleep unless he wishes it."

"Your parents did not come to you?" Angelina asked, trying and failing to keep that scandalized note from her voice.

"My provincial little bride." He sounded almost fond, though his dark gaze glittered. "That is what nannies are for, of course. My parents held regular audiences with the staff to keep apprised of my progress, I am told. But Castello Nero is no place for sticky hands and toddler meltdowns. I would be shocked to discover that your parents' shoddy little *château* was any different."

That was a reasonable description of the house, and still she frowned. "My parents were not naturally nurturing, certainly," Angelina said, choosing her words carefully. "But they were present and in our lives."

"No matter what, you need only call and I will come to you," Margrete had said fiercely before the wedding ceremony today. It had shocked her.

But Margrete had always been there. She might have been disapproving and stern, but she'd always been involved in her daughters' lives. Some of Angelina's earliest memories involved reading quietly at her mother's feet, or laboriously attempting to work a needle the way Margrete could with such seeming effortlessness.

It had never occurred to her that she would ever look back on her childhood fondly.

Of all the dark magic Benedetto had worked in the last month, that struck Angelina as the most disconcerting. Even as he towed her down yet another hall festooned with frescoes, priceless art, and gloriously thick rugs.

"You will find a variety of salons, an extensive private library, and an entertainment center along this hall." Benedetto nodded to doors as he passed them. "Any comfort you can imagine, you will find it here."

"Am I to be confined to this hall?"

"The castle is yours to explore," her husband said. "But you must be aware that at times, the castle and grounds are open to the public. Signora Malandra leads occasional tours. Because of course, there is no shortage of interest in both this castle and its occupant."

"But..."

Once more, she didn't know what on earth she meant to say.

Benedetto's dark eyes gleamed as if he did. "Foolish, I know. But far be it from me not to profit off my own notoriety."

He paused in the direct center of the long hall that stretched down the whole side of the castle. There was a door there that looked like something straight out of the middle ages. A stout wooden door with great steel bars hammered across it.

"This door opens into a stairwell," Benedetto told her. He did not open the door. "The stairwell goes from this floor to the tower above. And it is the only part of the castle that is strictly forbidden to you."

"Forbidden?" Angelina blinked, and shifted so she could study the door even more closely. "Why? Is the tower unsafe?"

His fingers were on her chin, pulling her face around to his before she even managed to process his touch.

"You must never go into this tower," he said, and there was no trace of mockery on his face. No curve to that grim mouth. Only that blazing heat in his dark eyes. "No matter what, Angelina, you must never open this door."

His fingers on her chin felt like a fist around her throat.

"What will happen if I do?" she asked, her voice little more than a whisper.

"Nothing good, Angelina." The darkness that emanated from him seemed to take over the light pouring in from outside. Until she could have sworn they stood in shadows. At night. "Nothing good at all."

She felt chastened and significantly breathless as Benedetto pulled her along again. Hurrying her down the long corridor until they reached the far end. He led her inside, into a master suite that was larger than the whole of the family wing of her parents' house, put together. It boasted a private dining room, several more salons and studies, its own sauna, its own gym, a room entirely devoted to an enormous bathtub, extensive dressing rooms, and then, finally, the bedchamber.

Inside, there was another wall of windows. Angelina had seen many terraces and balconies throughout the suite, looking out over the sea in all directions. But not here. There was only the glass and a steep drop outside, straight down into the sea far below.

There was a large fireplace on the far wall, with a seating area arranged in front of it that Angelina tried desperately to tell herself was cozy. But she couldn't quite get there. The fireplace was too austere, the stone too grim.

And the only other thing in the room was that vast, elevated bed.

It was draped in dark linens, gleaming a deep red that matched the ring she wore on her finger. *Like blood,* a voice inside her intoned.

Unhelpfully.

Four dark posts rose toward the high stone ceiling, and she had the sudden sensation that she needed to cling to one of them to keep herself from falling. That being in that bed, with nothing but the bloodred bedding and the sky and sea pressing down upon her, would make her feel as if she was catapulting through space.

As if she could be tossed from this chamber at any moment to her death far below.

Angelina couldn't breathe. But then, she suspected that was the point.

She only dimly realized that Benedetto had let go of her hand when she'd walked inside the room. Now he stood in the doorway that led out to the rest of the suite and its more modern, less stark conveniences.

Perhaps that was the point, too. That inside this chamber, there was nothing but her marriage bed, a fire that would not be lit this time of year, and the constant reminder of the precariousness of her situation.

And between her and the world, him.

"Is this where it happens, then?" She turned to look at him, and thought she saw a muscle tense in his jaw. Or perhaps she only wished she did, as that would make him human. Accessible. Possessed of emotions, even if she couldn't read them. "Is this where you bring your wives, one after the next? Is this where you make them all scream?"

"Every woman I have ever met screams at one point or another, Angelina," he said, and there was a kind of challenge in his gaze. A dark heat in his voice. "A better question is why."

But that impossible heat pulsed inside her, and Angelina didn't ask. She moved over to the bed and as she moved, remembered with a jolt that she was still dressed in her wedding gown. And between her legs, that pulsing desire he had cultivated in her thought it had all the answers already. She ran her hand over the coverlet when she reached it, not at all surprised to find that what she'd seen gleaming there in the dark red linens were precious stones. Rubies. Hard to the touch.

She pressed her palm down flat so that the nearest precious stone could imprint itself there. She gave it all her weight, as if this was a dream, and this was a kind of pinch that might jolt her awake.

Did she want to wake up? Or would it be better still to dream this away?

You keep thinking something can save you, something in her mocked her. *When you should know better by now.*

Angelina's palm ached, there where the hard stone dug into her flesh. And the man who watched her too intently from across the room was no dream.

She already knew too well the kind of magic he could work on her when she was wide awake.

Outside, she could hear the thunder of the sea. The disconcerting summer sky stretched off into the horizon.

But here in this castle filled with the plunder and fragments of long-ago lives, she was suspended in her white dress. Between the bloodred bed and the husband who stood like a wall between her and what remained of her girlhood. Of her innocence.

Whatever was left of it.

And suddenly, she wanted to tear it all off. She wanted to pile all the girlish things that remained inside her into that fireplace, then light a match.

Angelina was tired of being played with. She was tired of that dark, mocking gleam in his eye and that sardonic curve to his mouth. Of being led through a castle cut off from the mainland by a man who trafficked in nightmares.

She'd married him in a veil, but he had peeled it back when he claimed her mouth with his, there in front of witnesses.

She wanted to burn that down, too. No more veils of lace or ignorance.

If this was her life, or what remained of it, she would claim it as best she could.

She pressed her palm down harder on the coverlet, until it ached as much as she did between her legs.

Then Angelina faced the husband she couldn't quite believe was going to kill her like the rest. But she had to know if that was the real dream. Or a false sense of security six other women had already felt, standing right where she was now.

"I don't want to talk about screaming," she said.

He looked amused. "That is your loss."

"I have a question, Benedetto."

She thought he knew what she wanted to ask him. There was that tightening in his jaw. And for a moment, his black eyes seemed even darker than usual.

"You can ask me anything you like," he said.

She noticed he did not promise to answer her.

But Angelina focused on the question that was burning a hole inside her. "Don't you think it's time you told me what happened to the six who came before me?"

CHAPTER SEVEN

"AS YOU WISH," Benedetto said. His own voice was a rumbling thing in the bedchamber of stone, like thunder. Though outside it was a mild summer afternoon inching its way towards evening. "If you feel the shade of the marital bed is the place for such conversations."

He did not wish. He would prefer not to do this part of the dance—and he would particularly prefer not to do it with her.

The things he wanted to do with her deserved better than a castle made of unbreakable vows to dead men. She deserved light, not darkness. She deserved a whole man, not the part he played.

His still-innocent angel, who came apart so beautifully while the sea closed in around them. His curious Angelina, who would open doors she shouldn't and doom them both—it was only a matter of time.

His brand-new wife, who thought he was a killer, and still faced him like this.

Benedetto had expected her to be lovely to look at and reasonably entertaining, because she'd showed both at her dinner table the night they'd met. He had developed a deep yearning for her body over the course of the past month.

But he didn't understand how she'd wedged herself beneath his skin like this.

It wasn't going to end well. That he knew.

It never did.

And he had a feeling she was going to leave her mark in a way the others never had.

"Do you do the same thing every time?" she asked, as if she knew what he was thinking.

Benedetto couldn't quite read her, then. It only made him want her more. There was a hint of defiance in the way she stood and in the directness of her blue gaze. The hand on the wide bed shook slightly, but she didn't move it. Or hide it.

And he could see fear and arousal all over her body, perhaps more entwined than she imagined. He didn't share his father's proclivities. But that didn't mean he couldn't admire the things trembling uncertainty mixed with lust could do to a pretty face.

She tipped up her chin, and kept going. "Did you marry them all in bright white dresses, then bring them here to this room of salt and blood?"

It was a poetic description of the chamber, and he despised poetry. But it was also the most apt description he'd ever heard of what he'd done to this room after his grandfather had died. Benedetto had gutted it and removed every personal item, every hint of the man who'd lived and died here, every scrap that a ghost might cling to.

Because that was what he and his grandfather had done together after his grandmother had died, and it seemed only right to continue in the same vein.

And because he was haunted enough already.

"Where else would I bring them?" he asked softly.

"Tell me." Her gaze was too bright, her voice too urgent. "Tell me who they were."

"But surely you already know. Their names are in every paper, in every language spoken in Europe and beyond."

"I want to hear you say them."

And Benedetto wanted things he knew he could never have.

He wanted those nights in that stark conservatory in her father's ruined house, the wild tangle of music like a cloud all around them, and her sweetness in his mouth. He had wished more than once over this past month that he could stop time and stay there forever, but of all the mad powers people whispered he possessed, that had never been one of them.

And innocence was too easily tarnished, he knew. Besides, Benedetto had long since resigned himself to the role he must play in this game. Monster of monsters. Despoiler of the unblemished.

He had long since stopped caring what the

outside world thought of him. He had made an art out of shrugging off the names they called him. His wealth and power was its own fortress, and better still, he knew the truth. What did it matter what lesser men believed?

What mattered was the promise he'd made. The road he'd agreed to follow, not only to honor his grandfather's wishes, but to pay a kind of penance along the way.

"And who knows?" his grandfather had said in his canny way. With a shrug. *"Perhaps you will break your chains in no time at all."*

Benedetto had chosen his chains and had worn them proudly ever since. But today they felt more like a death sentence.

"My first wife was Carlota di Rossi," he said now, glad that he had grown calloused to the sound of her name as it had been so long ago now. It no longer made him wince. "Her parents arranged the match with my grandfather when Carlota and I were children. We grew up together, always aware of our purpose on this planet. That being that we were destined to marry and carry on the dynastic dreams of our prominent families."

"Did you love her?"

Benedetto smiled thinly. "That was never part of the plan. But we were friendly. Then they found her on what was meant to be our honeymoon. It was believed she had taken her own life, possibly by accident, with too many sleeping pills and wine."

"Carlota," Angelina murmured, as if the name was a prayer.

And Benedetto did not tell her the things he could have. The things he told no one, because what would be the point? No one wanted his memories of the girl with the big, wide smile. Her wild curls and the dirty jokes she'd liked to tell, just under her breath, at the desperately boring functions they'd been forced to attend together as teenagers. No one wanted a story about two only children who'd been raised in close proximity, always knowing they would end up married. And were therefore a kind of family to each other, in their way. The truth was Carlota was the best friend he'd ever had.

But no one wanted truth when there was a story to tell and sell.

Benedetto should have learned that by watching his parents—and their sensationalized deaths. Instead, he'd had to figure it out the hard way.

"Everyone agrees that my second wife was a rebound," he said as if he was narrating a documentary of his own life. "Or possibly she was the mistress I'd kept before, during, and after my first marriage."

He waited for Angelina to ask him which it was, but she didn't. Maybe she didn't want to know. And he doubted she would want to know the truth about the understanding he and Carlota had always had. Or how his second marriage had been fueled by guilt and rage because of it.

Benedetto knew his own story backward and forward and still he got stuck in the darkest part of it. In the man he'd allowed himself to become. A man much more like his detestable father than he'd ever imagined he could become.

When Angelina did not ask, he pushed on, his voice gritty. "Her name was Sylvia Toluca. She was an actress of some renown, at least in this country, and a disgrace to the Franceschi bloodline. But then, as most have speculated, that was likely her primary appeal. Alas, she went overboard on a stormy night in the Aegean after a well-documented row with yours truly and her body was never found."

"Sylvia," his new wife said. She cleared her throat. "And I find I cannot quite imagine you actually…rowing. With anyone."

Benedetto detached himself from the wall and began to prowl toward her. His Angelina in that enormous white gown that bloomed around her like a cloud, with those dark pearls around her neck and eyes so blue they made the Italian sky seem dull by comparison.

"I was much younger then," he told her, his voice a low growl. "I had very little control."

He watched her swallow as if her throat hurt. "Not like now."

"Nothing like now," he agreed.

She swayed slightly on her feet, but straightened, still meeting his gaze. "I believe we're up to number three."

"Monique LeClair, Catherine DeWitt, Laura

Seymour." Angelina whispered an echo of each of their names as he closed the distance between them. "All heiresses in one degree or another, like you. There were varying lengths of courtship, but yes, I brought each of them here once we married. All lasted less than three months. All disappeared, presumed dead, though no charges were ever brought against me."

"All of them."

He nodded sagely. "You would be surprised how many accidents occur in a place like this, where we are forever pitted against the demands of the sea. Its relentless encroachment." He stopped only scant inches from where she stood, reaching over to trace her hand where it still pressed hard against the bejeweled coverlet. "The tide waits for no man. That is true everywhere, though it is perhaps more starkly illustrated here."

"Surely, after losing so many wives to the sea, a wise man would consider moving inland," Angelina said in that surprising dry way of hers that was far more dangerous than the allure of her body or even her music.

Those only meant he wanted her. But this… This made him like her. "Or better still, teach them to swim."

"Do you know how to swim?" he asked, almost idly, his finger moving next to hers on the bed.

"I'm an excellent swimmer," she replied, though her color was high and her voice a mere whisper. "I could swim all the way to Rio de Janeiro and back if I wished."

He watched the way her chest rose and fell, and the deepening flush that he could see as easily on her cheeks as on the upper slopes of her breasts.

"I applaud your proficiency," he said. "But I am only a man. I can control very few things in this life. And certainly not an ocean or a woman."

She did not look convinced.

"And your last wife?" she asked, her breath sounding ragged as he began to trace a pattern from the hand on his bed up her arm, lazy and insinuating. "The sixth?"

"Veronica Fitzgibbon." Benedetto made a faint tsking sort of sound. "Perhaps the best-known of all my wives, before marrying me. You might even call her famous."

"More than famous," Angelina corrected him softly as his hand made it to the fine, delicate bridge of her collarbone and traced it, purely to make her shiver. "I doubt there's a person alive who cannot sing at least one of her father's songs. And then she dated his drummer."

"Indeed. Scandalous." He concentrated on that necklace of hers, then. The brooding pearls against the softness of her skin. The heat of her body, warming the stones.

"She lasted the longest. Three months and two days," Angelina whispered.

He made himself smile. "See that? You do know. I thought you might."

"She crashed her car into a tree," Angelina told him, though he already knew. He'd spent two days in a police station staring at the pictures of the wreckage as the authorities from at least three countries accused him of all manner of crimes. "On a mountain road in the Alps, though no one has ever been able to explain what she was doing there."

"There are any number of explanations," Benedetto corrected her. "Most assume she was fleeing me. And that I was hot in pursuit, which makes for a delicious tale, I think you'll agree." He lifted his gaze to hers. "Alas, I was giving a very boring lecture at a deeply tedious conference in Toronto at the time."

"And how will I go, do you think?" she asked, a different sort of light in her blue eyes, then.

He hated this. He had disliked it from the start, though a truth he'd had to face was that he'd found a certain joy in the details. The game of it. The end justifying the means. But here, now, with her and that bruised look on her face and his own heretofore frozen emotions unaccountably involved this time—he loathed it all.

"I have already told you," he said quietly. "We all die how we live. It is inevitable."

"But—"

"A better question to ask," he said quietly, cutting her off, "is why any woman would marry me, knowing these things. These assumptions and allegations that must be true, because they are repeated so often. There must be a fire after all this smoke, no? Why did you say yes, Angelina?"

He watched, fascinated, as goose bumps shivered to life all over her skin. And she shifted, there where she stood. "I had no choice."

"Will we be starting this marriage off with lies?" Benedetto shook his head. "Of course you had a choice. Your father promised me a daughter. Not you in particular. Had you refused to marry me I had two others to choose from."

"My mother made it very clear that none of us were permitted to say no, no matter what."

"That must be it, then." He didn't quite smile. It was too hard, too furious a thing. "But tell me, Angelina, how do you rationalize away the many times you came apart in my hands?"

"I don't rationalize it." Her blue eyes flashed. "I deplore it."

"I don't think you do," he told her, and he moved his hand to her jaw, tilting her head so that her mouth was where he wanted it. "I think you're confusing hunger for something else. But then, you did spend all that time in the convent, did you not? I'm surprised you feel anything at all save shame."

"I have a full complement of emotions, thank you. Chief among them, revulsion. Fury. Disgust."

"I want you too, little one," he said, there against her mouth. "I hear the seventh time is the charm."

She made a tiny little noise, protest and surrender at once, and then Benedetto took her mouth with his.

Because a kiss did not lie. A kiss was not a story told around the world, losing more and more truth each time it was sold to the highest bidder.

There was only truth here in the tangle of tongues. In the way her body shuddered beneath his hands. In the way she pressed herself against him, as if she would climb him if she could.

He could taste her fear and her longing, her need and her hope.

Benedetto tasted innocence and possibility, and beneath that, the sheer punch that was all Angelina.

He anchored her with an arm around her back, and bent her over, deepening the kiss. Taking more and more, until he couldn't be sure any longer which one of them was more likely to break.

She was intoxicating.

Despite all the times he'd done this, there had never been a time that he had wanted a wife like this. Or at all. But then, in all the ways that mattered, she was his first.

That thought made a kind of bitterness well in him, and he pulled away. And then took his time looking at her. Her lips parted. Her eyes dark with passion.

This from the woman who claimed she didn't want him at all. That she had been forced into this.

He rather thought not.

He liked to think he had been, though that wasn't quite true either. He'd had his choices, too.

"Not yet," he murmured, as much to himself as to her.

Because one choice he did have was to treat her the way he'd treated the others. He had already tasted her more than the rest of them, save Sylvia. He had already betrayed himself a thousand times over while in the thrall of her piano.

But she didn't have to know that. And he didn't have to succumb to it here.

And now that they were married, he could get this back on track.

Benedetto let go of her, pleased despite himself when she had to grip the bed beside her to stay on her feet. He picked up the hand she'd been pressing against the bed and could see the indentation of the coverlet's stone on her palm.

He was savage enough to like it.

"What do you mean, *not yet*?" she demanded. "I thought that once we were married—"

"So impatient," he taunted her. "Especially for one forced to the altar as you have been."

If she dared, he could tell, she would have cursed him to his face.

Instead, she glared at him.

"Don't you worry about consummating our

marriage." He laughed, though the lie of it caught a little in his chest. "I will take you in hand, never fear. But first, I wish to show you something."

Benedetto turned and headed for the door without taking her hand to bring her with him. And he smiled when he heard her follow him.

He didn't have to turn around and study her face to understand her reluctance. It was entirely possible she didn't know why she was following him. That she was simply as compelled as he was. He hoped so.

It was a good match for this mad yearning he felt inside, when he knew better. A yearning that he was terribly afraid would be the end of him. This innocent, untrained girl could bring him to his knees.

But then, that was a power he had no intention of handing over to her. If she didn't know, she couldn't use it.

He led her out into the master suite, then through a door that led to a separate tower from one of the salons.

Angelina balked at the door, looking around a little bit wildly.

"This is your tower," he told her, sounding almost formal. "You can enter whenever you wish."

"That seems like a lot of towers to remember," she said, a little solemnly, from behind him. "I wouldn't want to make a mistake."

He looked over his shoulder as they climbed the stairs.

"Don't," he warned her, and meant it more than he usually did. More than he wanted to mean it. "Whatever else you do here, do not imagine that the warning I gave you was a joke, Angelina."

He saw her swallow, hard, but then they were at the top of the stairs. He threw open the door, then waited for her to follow him inside.

And then Benedetto watched as she tried to contain her gasp of joy.

"A piano," she whispered, as if she couldn't believe it. "You really did get me a piano. A Steinway."

"I am assured it is the finest piano on the

Continent," he told her, feeling…uncertain, for once. Unlike himself. Did he crave her approval so badly? When he didn't care in the least if the entire world thought him a monster? It should have shamed him, but all he could do was drink in the wonder all over her. "It is yours. You can play it whenever you wish, night or day. And I will give instructions to my staff that you are to be left to it."

There was a look of hushed awe on her face. She aimed it his way, for a moment, then looked back at the piano that sat in the center of the room. When he inclined his head, she let out a breath. Then she ran to the piano to put her hands on it. To slide back the cover, and touch the keys.

Soft, easy, reverent. Like a lover might.

And for a deeply disturbing moment, Benedetto found himself actually questioning whether he was, in fact, jealous of an inanimate object.

Surely not.

He shoved that aside, because he'd been called a monster most of his life and he could live with the consequences of that. He had.

It was smallness and pettiness he could not abide, in himself or anyone else. Benedetto hated it in the men who auctioned off their daughters to pay their debts; he despised even the faintest hint of it in himself.

"Play, Angelina," he urged her. And if his voice was darker than it should have been, rougher and wilder, he told himself it was no more than to be expected. "Play for me."

He was married. Again. Every time he imagined he might be finished at last. That it would be the end of this long, strange road. That finally, this curse would be lifted and he would be freed.

Finally, he could bury his grandfather's dark prophecies in the grave where the old man lay.

And every time, Benedetto was proved wrong. He'd almost become inured to it, he thought as Angelina spread her fingers, smiled in that inward, mysterious manner that he found intoxicating, and began to coax something stormy and dark from the keys.

As the music filled the tower he admitted

to himself that this time he wanted, desperately, to be right.

He wanted to be done.

He wanted *her.*

It was the way she played, as if she was not the one producing the notes, the melodies, the whole songs and symphonies. Instead, it was as if she was a conduit, standing fast somewhere between the music in her head and what poured out of her fingers.

Benedetto had never seen or heard anything so beautiful.

And he couldn't help but imagine that she could do the same for him and the dark destiny he had chosen to make his own.

Outside, the afternoon wore on, easing its way into another perfect Italian evening.

And his bride played as if she was enchanted, her fingers like liquid magic over the keys. Half-bent, eyes half-closed, as if she was caught in the grip of the same madness that roared in him.

Or perhaps Benedetto only wished it so.

When *wishing* was another thing he had given up long ago.

Or should have.

But everything had changed when he'd walked into that dining room in her father's house and seen an angel where he'd expected nothing more than a collection of wan socialites. He stood against the wall in the tower room, his back against the stones that had defined him as long as he'd drawn breath.

It was easy to pretend that he had been disconnected from this place, shuttled off to boarding school the way he had been, but Castello Nero lived inside him and always had. As a child he'd loved coming home to this place. Endless halls, secret passages, and his beloved grandmother. His parents had always been away, but what did that matter when he could play mad siege games on the rocks or race the tide?

There was a part of him that would always long for those untroubled times. That wished he could somehow recreate them, if not for himself, for a child like the one he'd been too briefly. Maybe that was nothing more than a fantasy. Then again, maybe it was all he had.

He had to take his fantasies where he could.

Because it wasn't long after those dreamy days that he'd understood different truths about this place. These ancient walls and the terrible price those who lived here had paid, and would pay. Some would call it a privilege. Some would see only the trappings, the art and the antiques, the marble gleaming in all directions. Some would assume it was the shine of such things that made the difference.

They never saw any blood on their hands. They never heard the screams from the now defunct dungeons. They walked the halls and thought only of glory, never noticing the ghosts that lurked around every corner.

Or the ghosts that lived in him.

But as Angelina played, Benedetto imagined that she could see him.

The real him.

The music crashed and soared, whispered then shouted. The hardest part of him stood at attention, aching for her touch—and yet feeling it, all the same, in the music she played, here in the tower he had made a music room, just for her.

She played and played, while outside the

tide rose, the waves swelled, and the moon began to rise before the sun was down.

That, too, felt like a sign.

And when she stopped playing, it took Benedetto too long to realize it. Because the storm was inside him, then. *She* was. Her music filled every part of him, making him imagine for a moment that he was free.

That he could ever be free.

That this little slip of a woman, sheltered and sold off, held the key that could unlock the chains that had held him all his life.

It was a farce. He knew it was a farce.

And still, when she turned to look at him, her blue eyes dark with passion and need and all that same madness he felt inside him, he… forgot.

He forgot everything but her.

"Benedetto…" she began, her voice a harsh croak against the sudden, bruised silence.

"I know," he heard himself say, as if from a distance. As if he was the man he'd imagined he'd become, so many years ago, instead of the man he became instead. The man he doubted his grandmother would recognize. "I know, little one."

He pushed himself off from the wall and had the same sensation he always did, that the *castello* itself tried to hold on to him. Tried to tug him back, grip him hard, smother him, until he became one more stone statue.

Some years he felt more like stone than others, but not today.

But Angelina sat on the piano bench, her wedding gown flowing in all directions, and her chest heaving with the force of all the emotions she'd let sing through her fingers.

And she was so obviously, inarguably *alive* that he could not be stone. She was so vibrant, so filled with color and heat, that he could not possibly look down and find himself made into marble, no matter how the walls seemed to cling to him.

Benedetto crossed the floor, his gaze on hers as if the heat between them was a lifeline. As if she was saving him, here in this tower where no one was safe. And then he was touching her, his hands against her flushed cheeks, his fingers finding their way into the heavy, silvery mass of her blond hair.

At last, something in him cried.

"What are you doing?" she asked, though there was heat in her gaze.

"Surely you know," Benedetto said as he swept her up into his arms. "Surely your mother—or the internet—should have prepared you."

"Neither are as useful as advertised," she said, her head against his shoulder. And that dry note in her voice gone husky.

He had not planned to take her, as he had not taken the rest. They were offerings to fate, not to him. They were meant to worry over the bed that made his chamber look blooded, like so much stage dressing. They were never meant to share it with him. Not like this, dressed like a bride and at the beginning of this bizarre journey.

But Angelina was nothing like the others.

She never had been.

She was music, and she was light. She was every dream he'd told himself wasn't for him, could never be for him.

And every time he tasted her, he felt the chains that bound him weaken, somehow.

So Benedetto carried her, not down the tower stairs to the master suite, but to the chaise he'd set beneath the windows in this tower room. Because it had amused him to make this tower look as much like the conservatory in her father's shambles of the house as possible, he'd assured himself.

Or perhaps he'd done it because he wanted her to feel at home here, however unlikely that was—but he shied away from admitting that, even to himself. Even now.

He laid her down before him, admiring the way her hair tangled all about her. Like it, too, was a part of the same magic spell that held him in its thrall.

The same spell that made this feel like a real marriage after all.

"Welcome to your wedding night," Benedetto said as he lowered himself over her, and then he took her mouth with his.

Claiming Angelina, here in this castle that took more than it gave.

At last.

CHAPTER EIGHT

ANGELINA FELT TORN apart in the most glorious way and all he was doing was kissing her.

It was the music. The sheer excellence of the piano he'd found for her, and had set up in perfect tune.

She had only meant to play for a moment, but the keys had felt so alive beneath her fingers, as if each note was an embrace, that too soon, she'd lost herself completely.

She still felt lost.

And yet, somehow, she'd been aware of Benedetto the whole time. Her husband and perhaps her killer—though she couldn't quite believe that, not from a man who could give a piano like this as a gift—standing in the corner of the room with his gaze fixed on her.

She would not say that she was used to him, because how could anyone become used to a hurricane?

But she craved that electric charge. The darkness in his gaze, the sensual promise etched over his beautiful face, his clever mouth.

She'd played and played. And she could not have explained it if her life depended on it, as she supposed it might, but the longer she played, the more it was as if her own hands moved over her body. As if she was making love to herself, there before him, the way she had in the car.

Exposed and needy and at his command.

Right where she'd wanted to be since that very first night.

Angelina could hardly contain herself. All she could think of were the many times in this last, red-hot month of waiting and worrying and wondering, when her legs had been spread wide and he had been between them. His mouth. His fingers.

She'd played because her body felt like his already and there was no part of her that disliked that sensation.

She'd played because playing for him felt like his possession. Irrevocable. Glorious.

And as immovable as the stone walls of the tower that sang the notes she played back to her, no matter the piece, as sweet and sensual songs.

Benedetto lowered himself over her on the chaise, and she forgot about playing, because he kissed her like a starving man.

Angelina kissed him back, because his shoulders were as wide as mountains and behind him she could see only the darkening sky. And her ears were filled with the rushing sound of the sea waiting and whispering far below.

He was hard and heavy, and this time, he did not crawl his way down her body to bury his head between her legs. This time he let her feel the weight of him, pressing her down like a sweet, hot stone.

And all the while he kissed her, again and again, rough and deep and filled with the same madness that clamored inside her.

Angelina could no longer tell if she was still playing the piano, or if he was playing her, and either way, the notes rose and fell, sang and wept, and she could do nothing about it.

She didn't want to do anything about it but savor it.

Because whatever song this was, it made her burn.

Again and again, she burned.

Only for him, something in her whispered. And that made her burn all the more.

Benedetto tore his mouth from hers and began to move down her body, then, but only far enough to tug on the bodice of her dress. Hard.

He glanced at her, his dark eyes bright and gleaming, and tugged on her dress until it tore. Then he tore it even more, baring her breasts to his view.

And when she gasped at the ferocity, or at the surge of liquid heat that bloomed in her because of it, he laughed.

Benedetto looked at her, his face dark with passion and set fierce like a wolf's, as he shaped her breasts with those calloused palms of his and then took one aching nipple into his mouth.

And then she was a crescendo.

Angelina arched up, not sure if she was

fighting him or finding him, or both at the same time. His mouth was a torture and treat, and she pressed herself even more firmly into his mouth. Whatever he wanted to give her, she wanted to take. As much as possible.

His hands moved south, continuing their destruction. He tore her white dress to ribbons, baring her to him. And she thrilled to every last bit of sensation that charged through her from the air on her flesh, or better still, his wicked mouth.

And when he thrust his heavy thigh between hers even as he continued to hold her down and take his fill of her, she found that gave her something to rock the center of her need against.

Over and over again, because it felt like soaring high into the night.

And when she shattered, tossed over a steep edge as if from the window of this tower to the brooding sea far below, he laughed that same dark, delighted laugh that had thrilled her from the first.

Angelina could feel the laugh inside her, and it only made her shudder more.

When she came back to herself, rising from the depths somehow, he had rolled off of her. Her wedding dress was torn to pieces, baring her to his view completely. That he could see all of her was new, and faintly terrifying. No one had seen Angelina fully naked since she was a small child.

But far more overwhelming was the fact that as Benedetto stood beside her, looking down at the chaise from his great height, he was shrugging out of his own wedding clothes.

In all this time, all throughout this longest month, he had never dislodged his clothing or allowed her to do so.

"Are you horribly scarred?" she'd asked him once, feeling peevish with lust and longing and that prickling fear beneath. She'd been stretched out on her piano bench in the conservatory back home, after he'd buried his face between her thighs and made her scream.

As usual.

Benedetto had only smiled, drawing her attention back to that mouth of his and the things it could do. *"None of my scars are external."*

And now the first stars were appearing in the sky outside. He blocked them all out and somehow made them brighter at the same time, because he was perfect. He was everything.

She had never seen a naked man in real life. She had never imagined that all the various parts that she'd seen in pictures could seem so different in person. Because she knew what it felt like to be in his arms and she knew what it felt like to taste him in her mouth.

But Benedetto naked was something else. Something better. He looked as if he'd been fashioned by a sculptor obsessed with male beauty, but she knew that he would be hot to the touch. And more, unlike all the marble statues she'd ever seen—many of them here—there was dark hair on his chest. A fascinatingly male trail that led to a part of him she'd felt against her leg, but had never seen.

"What big eyes you have," he said, sounding dark and mocking.

Angelina jerked her gaze up over the acres

and acres of his fine male chest, all those ridges and planes that made her fingers itch. To touch. To taste. To make hers, in some way, the way he had already taken such fierce possession of her.

"I understand the mechanics," she confessed. "But still…"

"Your body knows what to do." He came down over her again, and she hissed out a breath because it was so much different, now. Bare flesh against bare flesh. Her softness against all the places where he was so impossibly hard. Everything in her hummed. "And so do I."

And then, once again, she felt as if she was the piano.

Because he played her like one, wringing symphonies out of her with every touch, every brush of his mouth over parts of her body she would have said were better ignored.

He flipped her over onto her stomach, right when she thought that she might simply explode out of her own skin—

And he laughed in that dark, stirring way of

his, there against the nape of her neck. Then he started all over again.

Angelina…lost track.

Of herself. Of him. Of what, exactly, he was doing.

All she could seem to do was feel.

He slipped his fingers between her legs and stroked her until she shattered and fell apart, but he didn't stop. There was no ending, no beginning. There was only the rise and fall. The fire that burned in both of them and between them, flickering one moment, then roaring to life the next.

And all the while Angelina couldn't seem to get past the feeling that all of this was exactly how it was supposed to be. All of this was *right*.

It was full dark outside when Benedetto turned her over again. He stretched her arms up over her head and finally, finally, settled himself between her thighs. She could *feel* him, a hard ridge of perfect male arousal where she was nothing but a soft melting.

She was shuddering. She thought maybe there was moisture on her face. But all Angelina could care about was the blunt head of his masculinity that she could feel pressing into her.

Not exactly gently. And yet not roughly, either.

It was a pinch she forgot about almost as soon as it happened followed by a relentless, masterful thrust, and then Benedetto was seated fully inside her.

And that time, when Angelina burst into flame and shattered into a million new pieces, each more ragged than the last, she screamed herself hoarse.

Benedetto was laughing again, dark and delirious and too beautiful to bear, as he finally began to move.

And all her notions about piano music and symphonies shattered.

Because this was far more *physical* than she could possibly have imagined. Her body gripped him. He worked himself into her, then out. His chest was a delicious abrasion against hers, she could feel the press of his hipbones with every thrust, and there was heat and breath and so much *more* than the things she'd read in books.

He dropped his hard, huge body against hers and Angelina thought that should smother her, surely. But instead she bloomed.

As if her body was made to be a cradle, to hold him between her thighs. Just like this.

He bent his head to hers and took her mouth again, so that she was being taken with the same sheer mastery in two places at once.

And she understood that there was no place he did not claim her.

Inside and out, she was his.

She could feel that ring of his on her finger and that hard male part of him thrust deep inside her body.

And it seemed to her that her pulse became a chant. *His. His.*

His.

And then, finally, Angelina tore her mouth from his. She gripped the fierce cords of his neck with her hands, and found herself staring deep into his dark, ferocious gaze.

Into eternity, she was sure of it.

His.

And when she exploded into fire and fury, claimed and reborn, he cried out a word that could have been her name, and followed.

Angelina was hardly aware of it when he moved. She came back to herself, disoriented and gloriously replete, as he lifted her up into his arms.

She was aware of it as he carried her down the tower's narrow stair, high against his chest with only her hair trailing behind them. As naked as the day they were born.

Maybe she should have been embarrassed, she thought idly. For she knew full well that just because a staff was unseen did not mean they were not witnessing the goings-on of the house.

But how could she care if there were eyes on them when she felt like this? More beautiful than she ever had been. Perfect in his arms.

Right, straight through.

And so she looped her arms around his neck, rested her head against his shoulder, and said nothing as he took her back to that master suite. She did nothing but *feel* as he carried her into that room she'd seen before that contained only a massive, luxurious tub with a view straight on to forever.

Benedetto put her down carefully beside it so she could hold on if her knees gave way. They did, and he smiled, and then he set about drawing the bath himself. Soon enough, the water was steaming. And the salts he threw in it give the water a silky feel when she dipped her fingers in.

He said nothing. He only indicated with his chin that she should climb into the hot water, so she did.

Then she sat there, relaxing against the sloping side, the warm water like an embrace. The heat holding her the way he had. She thought he would climb in with her, but instead, with a long, dark look she had no hope of reading, Benedetto left her there to soak.

Something curled around inside her, low and deep, so she stayed where she was to indulge it. The water felt too good. She was too warm, and outside the sea danced beneath the stars, and flirted with her. She could not bring herself to climb out.

Angelina didn't think she slept, there in a bathtub where she could so easily slip beneath the water to her death—in a place that hinted at death around every corner. But she was still startled when there were hands on her again, and she was suddenly being lifted up and out of the warm water.

But in the next moment, she knew it was him. And the knowledge soothed her.

It felt like a dream, so she didn't really react as Benedetto wrapped her in a towel and set about drying her himself. She had tied her hair in a knot on top of her head and she could feel the curls from the heat, framing her face, in a way she had never liked—but she did not have the energy to do anything about it.

She blinked, realizing that he had showered. She could smell the soap on him. And all he wore now were a pair of low-slung trousers. Somehow that felt more intimate than his nakedness.

For the first time, Angelina actually felt shy in this man's presence.

The absurdity did not escape her, after the things he'd done to her in her father's house. The things he'd done to her tonight. She should have been immune to him by now. Instead, he toweled her dry and then wrapped her in the softest, most airy robe she had ever felt in her life, and she suddenly felt awkward. Exposed.

She thought he would say something then. The way he looked at her seemed to take her apart, his dark eyes so unreadable and his mouth in that serious, somber line. But he didn't. He ushered her from the room, with a certain hint of something very nearly ceremonial that made her heart thud inside her chest.

"Where we going?" she asked.

And it was times like these, when she was walking next to him—close enough that they could have been hand in hand if they were different people—that she was more aware of him than was wise. How tall he was. How beautiful and relentlessly male.

How dark and mysterious, even though he wore so little.

And she was forced to confront the fact that it wasn't the things he wore that made him seem so dangerous. So outrageously powerful. It was just him.

The master of Castello Nero. The boogeyman of Europe.

Her husband. Benedetto.

"You did not think that was the sum total of your wedding night, I hope." There was the faintest hint of a smile on his hard face. "We have miles to go, indeed."

That didn't make her heart thud any less.

Angelina followed him down the hall inside the grand suite and noticed that all the doors stood ajar. All the doors in the castle were wide open, now that she thought of it, save the one he'd showed her out in the hallway.

She thought of reinforced steel and heavy oak. Hidden stairs to a secret tower.

And she didn't know why it made her pulse pick up.

"Do you live here now?" she asked. His brow arched, as if to say, *We are here, are we not?* She could almost hear the words and felt herself flush, ridiculously. But she pushed on. "I mean to say, after spending all that time in boarding school. And knowing that your own parents did not spend much time here, from what you said. When did you move back yourself?"

"After my grandfather died," he replied. Not in the sort of tone that invited further comments.

"Were these his rooms?"

But she already knew the answer. She eyed a portrait on the wall of an old man gripping a cane with a serpent's head as its handle, while staring down from his great height with imperious eyes that look just like Benedetto's.

"When I was young," Benedetto said, his voice sounding something slightly less than frozen through, "my grandfather entertained me for at least one hour every Sunday in his drawing room here. He asked me fierce and probing questions about my studies, my life, my hopes and goals, and then explained to me why each and every one of them was wrong. Or needed work."

He stopped at a different door, and beckoned for Angelina to precede him.

"He was a terrifying, judgmental, prickly old man who would have been a king in a simpler time. He was never kind when he could be cutting, never smiled when he could scowl, and I miss him to this day."

Angelina was so startled by the indication that Benedetto had emotions or feelings of any kind that she almost stumbled on her way into the room. And it took her a moment to realize that the reason she didn't recognize it outright as the private dining room she'd seen when she'd first walked into the suite was because it was transformed.

There were candles lighting up the table, and clearly not, as in her parents' house, because of worries about an impending electric bill. Because out in the hallway, lights were blazing. The candles were here to set a mood.

The table was filled with platters of food. And not, she thought she drew closer, just any food. A feast. There were only two table settings, straddling the corner of the highly polished, deep mahogany table, but there was food enough for an army.

"This looks like..."

But she couldn't finish the sentence.

"It looks like a celebration, I hope," Benedetto said stiffly. He pulled out the chair that was clearly meant to be hers, and she almost thought she saw a hint of something like apprehension on his face. Could it be... uncertainty? Her heart stuttered. "I stole you away from your wedding reception. I offer this instead."

And suddenly, Angelina found the world around her little bit blurry. She sat in the chair he indicated, jolting slightly when her bottom found the chair beneath her because she was tender. Gloriously, marvelously tender between her legs.

He had given her a perfect piano and let her play, so that her introduction to her new life—her new home, her new status, her possible dark fate—was draped in a veil of music.

He had taken her down on that chaise and made a woman of her.

Her chest felt tight because he had made her

wedding feast, and her *heart*. Her traitorous, treacherous, giddily hopeful heart beat out a rhythm that was much too close to joy for the seventh wife of the Butcher of Castello Nero.

Angelina could only hope it wouldn't be the death of her.

Literally.

CHAPTER NINE

SHE DID NOT ask him directly if he'd killed his wives.

How they'd died, yes. Not whether or not he was guilty of killing them. Not whether he'd done the dark deeds with his own two hands.

And Benedetto couldn't decide, as they sat and ate the wedding feast he'd had his staff prepare for them, if he thought that was evidence that she was perfect for him or the opposite.

All he knew was that he was in trouble.

That he had already treated her differently than any other woman, and all other wives.

He kept expecting something—anything—involving this woman to be *regular*. Ordinary. But instead, she was incomparable to anyone or anything, and he had no idea what to do with that.

Even now, when she was scrubbed clean,

bathed so that all her makeup was gone and her hair was merely in a haphazard knot on the top of her head, she was more radiant than she had been at their wedding ceremony.

And he didn't think he could bear it.

"You look quite angry with your crab cakes," she pointed out in that faintly dry tone of hers. "Or is it the company that does not suit?"

"Tell me about the piano," he said, instead of answering her question. "You are quite talented. Why did you never think to leave that ruin of a *château* and do something with it?"

"I thought of nothing else." And she actually grinned at him. At *him*. "There was no money for necessities, much less ambition."

"I do not understand," Benedetto said, with perhaps more ill-temper than necessary. "Surely your father could have avoided most of the unpleasantness in his life if he had made money from you and your piano. Rather than, say, trying his hand at high stakes card games he was doomed to lose before he walked in the room."

And this woman, this unexpected angel

who should never have agreed to become his wife, grinned even wider.

"But to do so, you understand, he would first have to believe that that infernal racket I was forever making could benefit him in some way. Instead, he often asked me why it was I could not entertain myself more quietly while sucking off the family teat, quote unquote. The way my sisters did."

Benedetto couldn't keep his eyes off of her. She was grinning as she waved away her father's indifference to her talent. And while she did, she applied herself to each course of the feast he had ordered with equal abandon.

He liked her hunger. He wanted to feed it.

All her hungers.

"It sounds as if you were kept in a prison," he told her, his voice in a growl. "But you do not seem the least bit concerned by this."

"Because you freed me."

And there was laughter in her voice as she said it. In her eyes, too, making the blue into a sparkle that was brighter than the candles.

A sparkle that faded the longer she gazed at him.

"It is a long, long time indeed since I have been viewed as the better of two options," he said darkly.

"People always tell you the devil you know is better," Angelina said, a wisdom beyond her years where that sparkle had been, then. "But I have never thought so. There's more scope for growth in the unknown. There has to be."

"How would you know such a thing? Did they teach it in the convent?"

Again, her lips moved into something wry. "Ask me in three months and two days or so."

And despite himself, Benedetto laughed.

What was the harm in pretending, just for a little while, that this was real? That it could be precisely what it seemed. No more, no less. Would that really be the worst thing that ever happened?

He suspected he knew the answer. But he ignored it.

When they finished eating, he led her out onto one of the balconies, this one equipped with a fire pit built into the stone, benches all around, and a hot tub on one end with nothing before it but the sea. He could imagine winter nights in that tub, the two of them wound around each other—

But he stopped himself, because she wouldn't be here when winter came.

He watched as she stood at the rail, the sea breeze playing with her hair, making it seem more like spun silver than before.

Or making him feel like spun silver himself, which should have appalled him.

"You look remarkably happy." The words felt like a kind of curse as they came out of his mouth. As if he was asking for trouble. Or tempting fate too directly, standing there beside her. It was as if his heart seized up in his chest, then beat too hard, beating out a warning. "Particularly for a woman who married a monster today."

She turned her dreamy face to his and then his fingers were there, helping the breeze at its work, teasing her hair into curls and lifting them seemingly at random.

"If you think about it," she said softly, "we are all of us monsters. In our hearts, most of all."

"Are you already forgiving me?" Benedetto asked, though it seemed to him that the world had gone still. The tide had stopped turning, the planet had stopped spinning, and there was only Angelina. His last, best wife and her gaze upon him, direct and true, like his own north star. "Don't you think that might be premature?"

"Do you need forgiveness?"

Something inside him crumbled at that. It was a question no one had ever asked him. Because everyone thought they already knew all the answers to the mystery that was Benedetto Franceschi. Everyone believed they were privy to the whole story.

Or they preferred to make up their own.

Over and over again.

"Carlota," he heard himself say. And though he was horrified, he couldn't seem to stop himself. "I should never have married her."

Angelina's gaze moved over his face, but he didn't see the revulsion he expected. Or anything like an accusation. It made him…hurt.

"I thought you had to marry her." She tilted her head slightly. "Isn't that what you said?"

"That was the understanding, but I doubt very much we would have been marched down the aisle with shotguns in our backs if we'd refused." He let go of her hair and straightened from the rail. And no matter how many times he asked himself what he thought he was doing, he couldn't seem to stop. "Still, we were both aware of our duty. I thought she was like me—resigned to our reality, but happy enough to play whatever games we needed to along the way. Because as soon as the line was secure, we could do as we liked. And even before, for that matter. All that needed to happen was that we set aside a certain period of time of strict fidelity to ensure paternity."

"That sounds very dry and matter-of-fact. We are talking about sex and marriage and relationships, are we not?"

"We are talking about ancient bloodlines," Benedetto replied. "Ancient bloodlines require ancient solutions to problems like heirs. And once the deed was done, we could carry on as we pleased. Another grand old tradition."

Angelina blinked. "You do know that science exists, don't you? No need to do the deed at all."

He should have stopped talking. He shouldn't have started. But he didn't stop.

"You must understand, Angelina. Carlota and I knew we were to be married before either one of us had any idea what that meant. We were intended for each other, and everything we learned about the opposite sex we learned in the shadow of that reality. And when it finally came time to do our duty, she suggested we jump right in and get the heir taken care of, rather than messing about with invasive medical procedures we would inevitably have to discuss in the press. We were friends. We were in it together. She rather thought we should handle things the old-fashioned way because it was quicker and easier. Theoretically."

"What did you think?"

There was a certain gleam in her gaze then that reminded him that this was a woman he'd not only married, but had enjoyed for the past month. And just today, had made sob out his name like another one of her symphonies.

Benedetto smiled. "I was young and brash and foolish. I thought that as long as Carlota and I had agreed on all the important things—like the fact neither one of us was interested in fidelity once our duties were handled, hale, and hardy—we might as well."

He could remember Carlota's bawdy laugh. The way she'd smoked cigarettes with dramatic, theatrical flourish. The way she rolled her eyes, speaking volumes without having to speak a word.

I can't cope with having it all hanging there over my head, she'd declared a few months before their wedding. It will be just be too tedious. Let's get in, get out. Get it done.

Are we a sports team? Benedetto had asked dryly.

In his memory, he was as he was now. Cynical. Self-aware and sardonic. But the reality was that he'd been twenty-two. Just like her. And he'd had no idea how quickly things could change. Or how brutally life could kick the unwary, especially people like them who thought their wealth protected them from unpleasant realities.

They'd both learned.

"I was so arrogant," he said now, shaking his head. "I was so certain that life would go as planned. Looking back, there were any number of warning signs. But I saw none of them."

"Was she very depressed?" Angelina asked, her eyes troubled.

"Carlota? Depressed? Never." Benedetto laughed. "She was in love."

"With you." Those blue eyes widened. "So you did break her heart when you refused to give up your mistress."

"That is a very boring tabloid story." Benedetto sighed. "Sylvia was my mistress, though I think you will find that when a man is twenty-two years old and dating an actress of roughly the same age, they're just…dating. But no matter, that does not make for splashy, timeless headlines."

"Mistress is certainly catchier," Angelina said quietly.

"Carlota was in love, but not with me," he

said, because he couldn't seem to stop doing this. Why was he doing this? Nothing good could come of unburdening himself to her. "He was not of our social class, of course. Her parents would not have cared much if she carried on with him, because everyone could boast about sleeping with the odd pool boy—which is something her mother actually said to me at her funeral. But you see, Carlota wasn't simply sexually involved with this man of hers. She was head over heels in love with him, and he with her. Something I knew nothing about."

And then he hissed in a breath, because Angelina lifted a hand and slid it over his heart.

"It works, Benedetto," she said quietly. "I can feel it."

He felt something surge in him, huge and vivid. Something he could hardly bear, and couldn't name, though he had the terrible notion that it had been frozen there inside him all this time. That it was melting at last.

And the only thing this was going to do was make this worse. He knew that all too well.

"We spent the first few days of our honeymoon as friends, because that was what we'd always been," he gritted out, because he'd started this. And he would finish it, no matter the cost. "But then she decided that we might as well start making that heir as quickly as possible, so we could move on. She went off to prepare herself. Which, because she was in love with another man and had never had the slightest interest in me, involved getting drunk and then supplementing it with a handful of pills."

"You don't think she killed herself," Angelina breathed.

"On the contrary," Benedetto said grimly. "I know she did. It was an accident, I have no doubt, but what does that matter? It happened because she needed to deaden herself completely before she suffered a night with me."

He had never said anything like that out loud before in his life. And he hated himself for doing it now. He wanted to snatch the words back and shove them down his throat. He wanted to insist that Angelina rip them out of her ears.

"Was she truly your friend?" Angelina

asked, and he couldn't understand why she wasn't looking at him with horror, as he deserved.

Or with the same resigned bleakness his grandfather had.

"She was," he said, another thing he never spoke about. To anyone. "She really was."

"Then, Benedetto." And Angelina's voice was soft. "You must know that she would never want you to suffer like this. Not for her. Don't you think she would have wanted at least one of you to be free?"

That landed in his gut like a punch.

He wasn't sure he could breathe.

"You have no idea what you're talking about, Angelina. You have no idea the kinds of chains—"

But he cut himself off, because that wasn't a conversation he could have, with her or anyone else. He'd promised. He'd chosen. He gathered her to him instead, then crushed his mouth to hers, pouring it all into another life-altering kiss.

For a moment, he imagined that it really could alter his life instead of merely *feeling* that way. That he could change something. Anything.

He kissed her and he kissed her.

And Benedetto realized with a surge of light-headedness that the taste he hadn't been able to get enough of over the past month, that impossible glory that was all Angelina, was hope.

Damn her, she was giving him *hope.*

He sensed movement in his peripheral vision, so he lifted his head, holding Angelina close to him so he could see who moved around in the dining room on the other side of the windowed doors.

It was Signora Malandra, and he felt himself grow cold as the older woman stared out at him.

She didn't say a word. But then, she didn't need to. Because if this castle was a prison, then Signora Malandra was the jailer, and it was no use complaining about a simple fact.

Angelina didn't see the silent, chilly exchange. Benedetto checked to make sure, and when he looked up again the housekeeper had disappeared.

Taking his fledgling hope with her.

"You don't have to tell me anything further," Angelina told him then. "You don't have to tell me anything at all, Benedetto."

Her face was still so perfect. Her expression still so dreamy. And he knew that she had forgiven him for acts she knew nothing about, even if that was something he could never do himself.

He swept her up into his arms again. And he didn't head for that bloodred bed in the room of stone that might as well have been a stage.

Benedetto shouldn't have done any of the things he'd done with Angelina, but he had. And he wasn't going to stop until he had to. But that only meant he needed to make sure what stolen moments they had were real.

She was the only thing in his life that had ever been real, as far as he could tell, for a long, long time.

He carried her into one of the salons, this one with a fireplace and a thick, soft rug before it. He lay her down and then busied himself preparing the fire.

"I would have sworn that there was no way a man of your consequence would know how to light a fire," Angelina said, laughing again.

And what was he supposed to do with her when she kept laughing where any other woman would have been crying? Shivering with fear? Barring herself in a bathroom? All things other wives of his had done after Sylvia had died, and with far less provocation.

But then, he hadn't touched any of them.

He looked over his shoulder at her, incredulously, but she didn't seem to take the hint.

"The only reason I know how to do it is because we relied on fires for light and heat in my father's house," she confided. Merrily, even. "Necessity makes you strong or it kills you, I suppose. Either way, not something the great Benedetto Franceschi would ever have to worry about, I would have thought."

He busied himself with the logs. "It was not always in my best interests to alert members of this household as to my whereabouts. I can fend for myself. Inside the walls of the castle, anyway."

"But surely—"

But Benedetto was done talking.

"Quiet, little one," he growled, and then he crawled toward her, bearing her back down beneath him.

And he taught her everything he knew.

How to take him in her mouth. How to indulge herself as if he was her dessert. How to ride him and how to drive him wild by looking over her shoulder with that little smile of hers while he took her from behind.

He was a man possessed, falling asleep with her there before the fire, only to wake up and start all over again.

He could not taste her enough. He could not touch her enough.

As if, if he only applied himself, he could take all that hope and beauty, all that magic and music, and infuse it directly into his veins.

As if there was more than one way to eat her alive.

As if he could keep her.

And in the morning, dawn crept through the

windows, pink and bright. It woke him where he lay stretched out before that fire still.

He had done everything wrong. He knew that.

But that didn't change what had to happen now. It didn't alter in the slightest the promises he'd made. The choices he'd walked into with his eyes wide open, never expecting this. Never expecting Angelina.

Benedetto lifted her up. He tried to steel himself against the way she murmured his name, then turned to bury her face against his shoulder, not quite waking up.

He carried her through the suite, everything in him rebelling as he walked into the bedchamber at last. Outside the windows, he could see the light of the new day streaking over the sea.

It should have been uplifting, but all he wanted to do was rage. Hit things. Make it stop.

He took her to that bloodred bed and laid her in it. He drew the coverlet up, but left her hand exposed, that bloodred ruby marking her as his. And a fortune or two of them surrounding her.

Blood on blood.

He didn't want to leave, but he knew he had no choice if he was to keep his old vow. He handled the hateful practicalities and then he tore himself away. He forced himself out of the bedchamber and refused to allow himself to look back.

But the sight of her was burned into his brain anyway. Blond hair spread out over the pillows like silver filigree, somehow making all that dark red seem less ominous. Cheerful, almost.

As if she really was an angel.

Benedetto took a long shower, but that didn't make it any better. He dressed in a fury, then had another fight on his hands to keep himself from walking back into the bedchamber and starting all over again.

Instead, he stepped out into the hall. He wasn't the least bit surprised to see the figure of his housekeeper waiting there, halfway down. Right in front of the door he'd told Angelina she was never to open.

Inside him, he was nothing but an anguished howl. But the only sound he made was that of his feet against the floor.

Walking toward his duty and his destiny, as ever.

When he reached Signora Malandra, they stared at each other for a quiet eternity or two.

"It is done," Benedetto said, the way he always did.

The older woman nodded, her canny gaze reminding him of his grandfather.

Or maybe that was his same old guilt talking too loudly once again, trying to drown out that tiny shimmer of hope.

"Very well then, sir," she said. She smiled at the door, locked tight, then at him. "So the game begins. Again."

CHAPTER TEN

ANGELINA WOKE UP on the first morning of her married life with a buoyancy inside her chest that she would have said was impossible—because she'd certainly never felt anything like it before.

At first, she was a bit surprised to find herself in that great, blood colored bed. More than surprised—she was taken aback that she had no memory of getting into it. The memories she did have were white hot, stretched out in front of a fire her forbiddingly grand husband built himself. A delicious shiver worked its way over her body, inside and out.

She sat up slowly, holding the bejeweled coverlet to her chest as she looked around. But nothing had changed. The room was still a stark aerie, nothing but stone before her and above her, and the sea outside. Waiting.

But for some reason, what she'd expected

would feel like a fall to her death felt like flying instead. Exhilarating. She shoved her hair back from her face, and spent a good long while staring out at the sea in the distance. Blue. Beautiful.

Only as brooding as she made it.

When she swung her legs over the side of the high bed and found the cool stones beneath her feet, she felt almost soothed. Not at all the reaction she would have expected to have in this room that had scared her silly yesterday.

She took a long, hot shower, reveling in such a modern installation only yards from that medieval bedchamber. And as she soaped herself up, reveling in how new her own skin felt, she thought that Benedetto was much the same as this castle of his. Stretched there between the old and the new and somehow both at once.

Benedetto.

Her heart seem to cartwheel in her chest, and she couldn't help the wide, foolish smile that took over her face at the thought of him. He had taken her virginity—or more accurately, she'd given it to him. First while she played, offering him everything she was, everything she had, everything she hoped and dreamed.

The physical manifestation of the music she'd played for him had been appropriately epic.

She could still feel his hands, all over her flesh. She could feel the tug and rip of her gown as he'd torn it from her, then buried himself inside her for the first time. She still shuddered as images of the darkly marvelous things he'd taught her washed through her, over and over.

And she couldn't wait to do all of it again.

Maybe, just maybe, she could be the wife who stuck.

She was turning that over in her head, thinking about stories that lost more truth in each telling, as she dressed herself in the sprawling dressing room that was filled with clothes that she knew, somehow, would fit her perfectly. Even if they bore no resemblance to the meager selection she'd brought herself. And she remembered, against her will, what Petronella had said. That two or three lost wives could be a tragedy, but add another three on top of that and there had to be intention behind it.

That, or Benedetto Franceschi, the least hapless man she had ever met, was just… profoundly unlucky.

A notion that made her laugh a little as she found her way out of the dressing room, following her nose. Coffee, if she wasn't mistaken. And she could feel excitement and anticipation bubbling inside of her, as if she was fizzy from the inside out, because she couldn't wait to see him again. His dark, forbidding face that she knew so much better now. That she'd kissed, touched. That she'd felt on every inch of her skin.

Between her legs, she felt the deep pulse of that hunger she would have said should surely have been sated by everything they'd done the night before.

But it seemed her husband left her bottomless.

Her husband, she repeated to herself. Giddily, she could admit.

She pushed the door open to one of the pretty little salons, expecting to see Benedetto there, waiting for her in all his formidable state. But instead, the dour housekeeper waited there with a blank expression on her dolorous face.

Or an *almost* blank expression. Because if Angelina wasn't mistaken, there was a glitter in Signora Malandra's too-dark eyes. It looked a little too much like triumph.

Angelina didn't like the trickle of uneasiness that slipped down her back.

"Good morning," Angelina said, sounding as frosty as her own mother. She pulled the long, flowing sweater she'd found more tightly around her, because it might be the height of summer out there, but old castles were cold. All that stone and bloody history, no doubt.

"I trust you slept well," the older woman said, lifting an accusing eyebrow in a manner Angelina was all too familiar with. "If... deeply."

This woman could not possibly be attempting to shame her master's brand-new wife because she'd slept half the morning away. After her *wedding night*. Surely not.

"Have you seen my husband?" Angelina asked instead of any number of other things she might have said. Because if Margrete had taught her anything, it was that a chilly composure was always the right answer. It made others wonder. And that was far better than showing them how she actually felt.

Signora Malandra indicated the small table near a set of French doors that stood closed, no doubt to control the sea air. And then waited there, gazing back at her, until Angelina realized the woman had no intention of answering her until she obeyed.

Luckily, Angelina had spent her entire life under the thumb of overly controlling women. What was one surly housekeeper next to her mother and sisters? So she only smiled, attempted to look meek and biddable, and went to take her seat. As ordered.

Her act of rebellion was to crack open one of the doors, and then she smiled as the breeze swept inside, fresh and bright.

"Coffee?" the older woman asked. It sounded like an accusation.

Angelina channeled her mother and smiled wider, if more icily. "Thank you for asking. The truth is, I don't care for much in the way of breakfast. I like my coffee strong and very dark, and sometimes with a bit of cream. But only sometimes. I don't like anything to interfere with my walk."

"And where will we be walking?" the housekeeper asked as she poured Angelina a cup of coffee. "Perhaps we have forgotten that this is an island. The castle covers the whole of it, save a few rocks."

It took everything Angelina had not to respond to that. Not to point out that *we* were not invited.

The other woman sniffed as if she'd spoken aloud. "Though I suppose if you are feeling enterprising, you could walk the causeway. It's quite a pretty walk, though I'm not sure I would attempt it until I became more conversant with the tides."

"What a wonderful idea," Angelina said with a sweetness she did not feel. And when she took a sip of the coffee, it was suitably bitter. Which matched her mood.

"I was born and raised in this castle," Signora Malandra said, and again, Angelina could see something she didn't quite like in the older woman's gaze. "It sounds like foolishness, to warn every person who visits here about the inevitability of the tide when the ocean is all around us. But I warn you, mistress." And there was an inflection on that word that made Angelina's stomach tighten. "This is not a sea to turn your back on."

Angelina felt chilled straight through, and it had nothing to do with the breeze coming in from the water. She was glad she'd thought to wrap the sweater around her when all she wore beneath was a light, summerweight dress that she'd chosen because the color—a bright pop of yellow—made her happy.

She did not feel quite so happy now.

And she did not appreciate having dour old women try to scare her, either.

"My husband?" she asked again, as Signora Malandra looked as if she was headed for the door.

"Your husband is gone," the old woman said coolly. And again, with that hint of triumph in her gaze. "Did you not get what he left you?"

"What he left me?" Angelina repeated, not comprehending. How could Benedetto be *gone?* Did she mean…into town, wherever that was? She tried to conceal her shock. "Has he gone out for the day?"

And this time, there was no mistaking the look on the other woman's face. It was far worse than *triumphant.* It was pitying.

"Not for the day, mistress. Two months, I would say. At the very least."

And by the time Angelina had processed that, Signora Malandra was gone.

This time, when she found her way back into the bedchamber, it seemed ominous again. Altered, somehow. Almost obscene.

Someone had made up the bed in Angelina's absence, and that felt as sickening as the rest, as if some unseen evil was swirling around her, even now—

A sound that could have been a sob came out of her then, and she hated herself for it.

She remembered his face, out there on the balcony last night. That had been real. She was sure of it. Angelina had to believe that what she felt was real, not the rest of this. Not the stories that people had told, when the one he'd told her made more sense. Not because she wanted to believe him, though she did.

But because real life was complicated. It had layers and tragedies. It was never as simple as *a bad man*. It was never black and white, no matter how people wanted it to be.

There was nothing in the room, not even bedside tables, and she thought the housekeeper must have been playing with her.

Even as she breathed a little easier, however, she realized with a start that the mantel over the fire didn't look the way it should. She drifted closer to the fireplace, her heart in her throat, because there was a bit of paper there with an object weighting it down.

She could have sworn it hadn't been there when she woke up. Then again, her attention had been on that happiness within her that now felt curdled, and the watching, waiting sea.

Her whole body felt heavy, as if her feet

were encased in concrete as she moved across the floor. But then, at the last moment—almost as if she feared that someone would come up behind her and shove her into the enormous hearth if she wasn't careful—she reached out and swiped the paper and its paperweight up. Then moved away from the fireplace.

The object was a key. Big and ornate and attached to a long chain.

She stared at it, the weight of it feeling malevolent, somehow. Only when she jerked her gaze from it did she look at the thick sheaf of paper with a few bold lines scrawled across it.

This is the key to the door you must not open.

Benedetto had written that. Because of course, this was his handwriting. She had no doubt. It looked like him—dark and black and unreasonably self-assured.

You must wear the key around your neck, but never use it. Can I trust you, little one?

And for a long time after that, weeks that turned to fortnights and more, Angelina careened between disbelief and fury.

On the days that she was certain it was no more than a test, and one she could handily win, she achieved a kind of serenity. She woke in the morning, entertained herself by sparring with the always unpleasant housekeeper, and then tended to her walk. When the weather was fine, and the tide agreeable, she did in fact walk the causeway. Out there on that tiny strip of not quite land, she felt the way she did when she was playing the piano. As if she was simultaneously the most important life in the universe, and nothing at all—a speck in the vastness. The sea surged around her, birds cried overhead, and in the distance, Italy waited. Wholly unaware of the loneliness of a brand-new bride on a notorious island where a killer was said to live. When the man she'd married had been a dark and stirring lover instead.

Her husband did not call. He did not send her email. She might have thought she'd dreamed him altogether, but she could track his movements online. She could see that he was at meetings. The odd charity ball. She could almost convince herself that he was sending her coded messages through these photographs that appeared in the society pages of various international cities.

Silly girl, she sometimes chided herself. *He is sending you nothing. You don't know this man at all.*

But that was the trouble. She felt as if she did.

She didn't need him to tell her any more of his story. She knew—she just *knew*—that her heart was right about him, no matter what the world said.

Those were the good days.

On the bad days, she brooded. She walked the lonely halls of the hushed castle, learning her way around a building that time had made haphazard. Stone piled upon stone, this wing doubling back over that. She walked the galleries as if she was having conversations with the art. Particularly the hall of Franceschis past. All those dark, mysterious eyes. All those grim, forbidding mouths.

How many of them had locked their women away? Leaving them behind as they marched off to this crusade or that very important business negotiation, or whatever it was men did across time to convince themselves their lives were greater than what they left behind.

On those days, the portraits she found online of the stranger she'd married felt like an assault. As if he was taunting her from London, Paris, Milan.

And all the while, she played.

Her tower was an escape. The safest place in the castle. She played and she played, and sometimes, she would stagger to the chaise, exhausted, so she could sleep a bit, then start to play all over again.

And if she didn't know better, if food didn't appear at regular intervals, hot tea and hard rolls, or sometimes cakes and coffee, she might have imagined that she was all alone in this lonely place. Like some kind of enchanted princess in a half-forgotten fairy tale.

She played and she played.

And the weeks inched by.

One month. Another.

"Sweet God," said Petronella, when Angelina was finally stir crazy enough to call her parents' home. "I convinced myself he'd killed you already and was merely hiding the evidence."

"Don't be melodramatic," Angelina replied primly, because that was easier. And so familiar, it actually felt good. "He's done nothing of the kind."

Or not in the way that Petronella meant it, anyway. They put her on speaker, and she regaled her mother and sisters with tales of the castle. She'd tagged along on enough of Signora Malandra's tours by then that she could have given them herself, and so spared no flourish or aside as she shared the details of the notorious Castello Nero with her family.

Because she knew they would think wealth meant happiness.

Because to them, it did.

"Everywhere I look there's another fortune or two," she assured her mother. "It's really spectacular."

"I should hope so," Margrete said, in her

chilliest voice. "That was the bargain we made, was it not?"

And when she hung up, Angelina was shocked to find herself...sentimental. Nostalgic, even, for those pointless nights huddled together in the drawing room of the dilapidated old *château*, waiting to be sniped at and about. Night after night after night.

Who could have imagined she would miss that?

She would have sworn she could never possibly feel that way. But then again, she thought as she moved from one well-stocked library to the next—because the castle boasted three separate, proper libraries that would take a lifetime or two to explore—she was more emotional these days than she'd ever been in her life.

She'd woken up the other morning crying, though she couldn't have said why. She slept in that absurd bed every night, almost as if it was an act of defiance. But she couldn't say her dreams were pleasant. They were dark and red, and she woke with strange sensations in her body, especially in her belly.

Angelina was glad she couldn't remember the one that had rendered her tearful. Though the truth was, everything seemed to make her cry lately. Even her own music.

That night, she followed her usual routine. She played until her fingers hurt, then she staggered down the stairs from her tower to find a cold dinner waiting for her. She ate curled up on a chilly chair out on the balcony while the sea and wind engaged in a dramatic sort of dance in front of her. There was a storm in the air, she could sense it. Smell it, even.

When she could take the slap of the wind no longer, she moved inside. She was barefoot, her hair a mess, and frozen straight through when she left the master suite and walked down that hallway. The key he'd left her hung around her neck as ordered, the chain cool against her skin and the key itself heavy and warm between her breasts.

And she stood there, on the other side of that door, and stared at it.

Some nights she touched it. Other nights she pounded on it with her fists. Once she'd even gone so far as to stick the key into the lock, though she hadn't turned it.

Not yet.

"I am not Pandora," she muttered to herself.

As always, her voice sounded too loud, too strange in the empty hallway.

She had no idea how long she stood there, only that the world grew darker and darker on the other side of the windows, and she'd neglected to put on any lights.

When lightning flashed outside, it lit everything up. It seemed to sizzle inside of her like a dare.

A challenge.

It had been two months and three days. It was nearly September. And she was beginning to think that she had already gone crazy. That she was a madwoman locked away in a castle, which was an upgrade from the proverbial attic, but it ended up the same.

Alone and unhinged. Matted hair and too much emotion. And an almost insatiable need to do the things she knew she shouldn't.

There was another flash of lightning, and

then a low, ominous rumble of thunder following it.

She heard a harsh, rhythmic kind of noise, and realized with some shock that she was panting. As if she'd been running.

And then, when another roll of thunder seemed to shake that wall of windows behind her, she found herself sobbing.

Angelina sank to her knees, there in that solitary hall.

She had waited and waited, but it was nights like this that were killing her. Was this how he'd rid himself of all those wives?

And as soon as she had that thought, she had to ask herself—what kind of death was worse?

This had to be a test. But how long could she do it? She'd had a month of play, and then one impossibly beautiful night with a man everyone insisted was evil incarnate. Her heart had rejected that definition of him.

Could she set that against these months of neglect? She was slowly turning into one of the antiques that cluttered this place. Soon she would be nothing more than a story the dour old woman told, shuffling groups of tourists from room to room.

"I have been a prisoner my whole life," she sobbed, into her hands.

Her piano made her feel free, but she wasn't.

At the end of the day, she was just a girl in a tower, playing and playing, in the hopes that someone might hear her.

All Benedetto had done was trap her. Her family had never wished to listen to her play, but they'd heard her all the same. Now the only thing that heard her was the sea, relentless and uncaring. Waiting.

She lifted her head, shoving the mass of her hair back. Her heart was kicking at her, harder and harder.

She already knew what her mother would tell her. What her sisters would advise.

You've got it made, Petronella would say with a sniff. *You're left to your own devices in a glorious castle to call your own. What's to complain about?*

Angelina understood that she would fail this test. That she already had, and all of this had been so much pretending otherwise. The key suspended between her breasts seemed to pulse, in time with that hunger that she still couldn't do anything to cure.

Before she knew what she meant to do, the key was in her hand. She stared at it, as another flash of lightning lit up the hall, and she could have sworn that she saw the key flash too. As if everything was lightning and portent, dread and desire.

The ring Benedetto had put on her other hand seemed heavy, suddenly. And all she could think about was six dead women. And a bedchamber made bloodred with dark rubies.

And was she really to blame if she couldn't stay here any longer without looking behind the one door that was always kept closed?

What if he was in there? Hurt?

What if something far more horrible was in there?

Like all the women who had disappeared, never to be heard from again.

Even as she thought it, something in her

denied it. Her heart would not accept him as a villain.

But either way, she found herself on her feet.

And then she was at the door, one palm flat against the metal. She blew out a breath that was more like a sob. She thrust the key into the lock, the way she'd done one time before, amazed how easily it went in. Smooth and simple and *right*.

She held her breath. Then she threw the dead bolt.

Alarms didn't sound. The castle didn't crumble to ash all around her.

Emboldened, Angelina blew out the breath she was holding. She took another one, deeper than before, and pushed the heavy door open. She expected it to creak ominously, as if she was in a horror film.

But it opened soundlessly on a stair, very much like the one she climbed every day to her own tower.

Thunder rumbled outside, the storm coming closer. She couldn't see a thing, so she inched inside, then reached out her hand into the darkness, sliding it along the stone, her whole body prickling with a kind of premonition. Or fear. Panic that she would thrust her hand into something terrible—

But she found a light switch where she expected to, in the same place it was in her stairwell. She flicked it on and then began to climb.

Each step felt like a marathon. So she went faster and faster, climbing high, until she reached another door at the top. And her heart was beating too hard for her to stop now. There was too much thunder outside and in her, too.

She threw open the second door and stepped inside, reaching and finding another light and switching it on.

And then she blinked. Once, then again, unable to believe her eyes. Angelina dropped her hand to her side, drifted in a few more steps, and looked around as if she expected something to change…

But nothing changed.

It was an empty room with windows over the sea, just like the tower room she spent her days in. There were stone walls, a bare floor, and a high ceiling where a light fixture hung, illuminating the fact that there was nothing here.

Benedetto had demanded she stay out of an empty room.

That sparked something in her, half a laugh, half a sob.

Angelina thought she heard a noise and she jumped, expecting *something*... But that was the trouble. She didn't know what she wanted. And the room was empty. No monsters. No dead wives. No words scrawled on a paper, or carved into the stone. Just…nothing.

The same nothing these last two months had been.

That made something in her begin to throb, painfully.

She was disgusted with herself. She didn't know if she wanted to go play her piano until she felt either settled or too wound up to breathe, or if she should crawl beneath that heavy coverlet again to dream her unsettling dreams.

But when she turned around to go, she stopped dead.

Because Benedetto stood in the doorway to the empty chamber, the expression on his face a far more terrible thunder than the storm outside.

CHAPTER ELEVEN

BENEDETTO HAD STAYED away for six weeks. It was easy enough to do, touring his various business concerns. Such a tour would normally have claimed all of his attention, but this time he had found himself distracted. Unable to focus on what was in front of him because he was far more concerned with what he'd left behind.

That hadn't happened in as long as he could remember.

He wasn't sure it had ever happened. But that was Angelina. She was singular even when she wasn't with him.

And since his return to this castle he'd forgotten how to love the way he had as a child, he had become a ghost.

The irony wasn't lost on him. That he should be the one to haunt these old halls, staying in the servants' quarters and wandering in the shadows, both part of the castle and apart from it… Perhaps it was a preview of what awaited him.

Because the other option was that it was a memory of his time here when he was young and had seen the *castello* as his personal playground, magical and inviting in every respect, and that was worse, somehow.

But Angelina had cracked, as he'd known she would. He'd hoped her singularity would extend to this and she might be the one to resist temptation, but she didn't. None of them managed it. Sooner or later, they ended up right here in this empty room above the sea, staring at him as if they truly expected him to come in wielding an ax.

He had come to enjoy, on some level, that they believed all the stories they heard about him and married him anyway. The triumph of his wealth over their fear.

It wasn't as if any of them had touched him the way Angelina had. None of them had seen him, listened to him, or made love to him. None of them had played him music or treated him as if he was a man instead of a monster.

They had married his money. And they all came into this empty room, sooner or later, despite his request they stay away, expecting to come face-to-face with the monster they believed he was. The monster they *knew* he was.

Benedetto had long since stopped minding the way they looked at him when they saw him in the door, as if they could *see* the machete he did not carry with him.

This time, it hurt.

This time, it was a body blow.

"What are you doing here?" Angelina demanded. Her face was pale, her beautiful blond hair whipping around her with the force of her reaction. One hand was at her throat, and he could see the panic in her eyes.

If he was a better man, the fact that *her* fear pierced his soul would drop him, surely. And he would not stand here, wondering why it was that heightened emotion made her even more beautiful.

Or why it reminded him of the look on her

face when she'd shuddered all around him, again and again.

Or why nothing about her was like the others—and he *hated* that they were here in this room anyway. Playing out this same old scene. This curse of his he had chosen when he'd never imagined he would want to see the end of it, much less meet someone who'd made it—and him—feel broken from the start.

"Why should I not be here?" he asked, aware as he spoke that he was…not quite as in control of himself as he might wish. Not as in control as he usually was for this scene. "Perhaps you have forgotten that I'm the master of this castle."

"Now that you mention it, you do look vaguely familiar," she threw at him, any hint of fear on her face gone as if it had never been. Instead, she looked fierce. "You almost resemble a man I married, who abandoned me after one night."

"I did not abandon you." He spread his hands open before him. "For here I am, Angelina. Returned to you. And what do I discover but betrayal?"

"You ordered me to stay out of an empty room," she said, as if she couldn't believe it. The hand at her throat dropped to her side, and she took a step toward him, her blue eyes as stormy as the sea and sky outside. "Why would you do that? Do you know what I thought…?"

"But this is a room of terror, clearly," he taunted her, his voice dark, and it was less an act than it usually was. "Look closely, little one. Surely you can hear the screams of the women I've murdered. Surely if you squint, you can see their bodies, splayed out like some horrific art installation."

He watched her emotions move over her face, too quickly to read. And wished—not for the first time—that it was different.

Lord help him, but he had wished that she would be different.

"That is what you came for, is it not?" he demanded, his words an accusation.

"Are you trying to tell me that is not exactly what you wish me to think?" She waved one hand, the ring he'd put on her finger gleaming like the only blood in this room. "Is that what makes you happy?"

"I gave up on happiness a long time ago," Benedetto growled. "Now I content myself with living down to people's worst nightmares? Why shouldn't I? Everyone needs a villain, do they not?"

Angelina moved toward him, staggering slightly, her bare feet against the cold stone. "I do not want a villain, Benedetto. I want a husband."

"If that were true, you'd be asleep even now, tucked up in the marital bed. It would not have occurred to you to disobey me."

"What you are describing is a dog, not a wife," she snapped at him. "I never promised you obedience."

"Surely that was understood," he shot back. "When I bought you."

And again, he knew that he was far less in control of himself than he ought to have been. He had played this scene out before, after all. He usually preferred an iciness. A cool aloofness that wasn't an act, because it was his usual, normal state.

Nothing about Angelina had been normal or usual. Nothing about this was ordinary.

Even now he wanted to bundle her up into his arms and carry her off. And never, ever put her down again.

"Are you going to tell me what all of this is about?" she asked after a moment, when he'd found himself entirely too entranced by the way her jagged breaths made her body move.

He could see her cheeks were tearstained. She was the one who had disobeyed, the way they all disobeyed, and yet he felt as if *he* had betrayed *her*.

For moment he couldn't understand why.

And then it hit him.

For the first time since he'd met her, Angelina was looking at him as if he really might be a monster, after all.

Of all the things he'd lost, of all the indignities the choices he'd willingly made long ago required that he endure, it was this he thought might take him to his knees.

"Or are these just the kinds of games you

like to play?" Angelina asked when he only stared at her. She shook her head, swallowing hard, as if she was holding words back. Or a sob. Or, if that hectic look in her eyes was any guide, a scream. "I am so deeply sick and tired of being nothing more to anyone but a game piece to be moved around a board that is never of my choosing. Is this how you do it, Benedetto? Do you set up every woman you marry in the same way? Do you plot out the terms of your own betrayal, give them the key, and then congratulate yourself on having weeded out yet another deceitful bride? When all along it is you who creates an unwinnable situation?"

He eyed her, amazed that he felt stung by the accusation when he knew it was perfectly true—and more, deliberate. Yet no matter the sting, he was entranced by the magnificence of her temper that reminded him of nothing so much as the way she played that piano. In his weeks here as the resident ghost of his own lost childhood, he'd found himself listening to her play more than he should. He'd found himself sitting behind the stairs, losing himself on the notes she coaxed from the keys.

As if she'd still been playing for him.

Focus, he ordered himself.

"Am I the only one you made sure would fail?" Angelina demanded. "Or is this how you do it? And what do you gain from this? Do you toss us out a tower window, one by one?"

Benedetto laughed, though nothing was funny. "Would that suit your sense of martyrdom, wife?"

She stiffened. "I am no martyr."

"Are you not? Tell me, how else would you describe a young woman who was presented to a known murderer and allowed him a taste of her on that very first night? Do you also write to mass murderers in prison, offering your love and support? There are many who do. I'm sure the attendant psychological problems are in no way a factor."

She looked at him for what felt like a very long time, a kind of resolve on her face. "I didn't believe you were a murderer. I still don't."

And something in him rocked a bit at that. "Because you had made such an in-depth study of my character over the course of that one dinner?" He didn't like the emotion on her face then. He didn't like *emotion.* He growled. "Perhaps, as we are standing here together, stripped down to honesty in this empty room, we can finally admit that what you truly wanted was to escape. And all the better if you could do it while hammered to the family cross."

"Surely a martyr is what you wanted," she replied, displaying that strength he'd heard in her music time and time again. And quietly. "Or why would you go to such trouble to present yourself as a savior, willing to haul a family like mine out of financial ruin—but only for a price."

"I know exactly why it is I do what I do," Benedetto growled with a soft menace. "A better question is why you imagined you could marry a man like me, surrender yourself to my dark demands, and have things end differently for you than the rest. Do you truly imagine yourself that special, Angelina?"

"I don't know," she said, and there was something in her gaze then. A kind of knowing on her lovely face that clawed at him like the storm outside, thunder and flashes of light. "But there were times you looked at me and it seemed clear that you thought so, Benedetto."

She could not have pierced him more deeply had she pulled out a knife and plunged it into his heart. Then twisted it.

Benedetto actually laughed, because he hadn't seen it coming. And he should have. Of course he should have.

Because there was nothing meek about his Angelina. His angel. She was all flaming swords and descents from on high in a blaze of glory, and if he hadn't understood that when he had first seen her—well. When she'd played for him that first night, it had all been clear.

Then he'd tasted all that flame himself.

And there was no coming back from that.

She had introduced music into his life. Now it would live in him, deep in his bones no matter where in the world he went, and he had no idea how he was going to survive without it.

Or without her.

Because these last two months had been torture. If they had been a preview of what awaited him, he might as well chain himself up in his own dungeon and allow himself to go truly mad at last.

It almost sounded like a holiday to him.

"Are you going to kill me?" she asked, and despite the question, she stood tall. She didn't try to hide from him. After a beat he realized there was no fear on her face. "Is that the truth of you, after all?"

And this was the life he had chosen. He had made a promise to his grandfather years ago, and time after time he had kept it.

He had considered it a penance. He had taken a kind of pride in being so reviled and whispered about on the one hand, yet courted and feted all the same because no matter what else he was, he was a man of a great and historic fortune.

Benedetto had considered it a game. For what did he care what names he was called?

Why should it matter to him what others said? He had yet to meet anyone who wouldn't risk themselves in his supposedly murderous presence if it meant they would get paid for their trouble.

He had cynically imagined he understood everything there was to know about the world. He had been certain he had nothing left to learn—that nothing could surprise him.

He understood, now it was too late, that the point of it all had been a woman like Angelina.

It was possible his grandfather had expected someone like her to come along sooner, so that Benedetto would learn his lesson. It had never been a game or a curse. It had been about love all along.

Love.

That word.

Franceschis do not love, his mother had told him with one of her bitter trills of laughter. *They destroy.*

Love yourself, his father had said as if in agreement, his tone mocking in response to his wife. He'd cast a narrow sort of look at his only son and heir. *No one else will. Not because Franceschis destroy, or any such superstition. But because the only thing anyone will ever see is your fortune.*

He loves me, Carlota had told him on the day of their wedding. *He knows me. And so he also knows that my duty to you must come first.*

She was joy and she was love, his grandfather had said stiffly on the morning of his grandmother's funeral, staring out at the sea. *And none of each can possibly remain without her.*

I love you, Benedetto, his grandmother had told him long, long ago, when she'd found him hiding in one of the *castello*'s secret passageways. *I will always love you.*

But always had not lasted long.

As far as he had ever been able to tell, love had died along with her, just as his grandfather had said.

Something he'd been perfectly happy with all these years.

Until now.

When it was too late.

Because he knew how this scene between them was about to go. He played the monster and his wives believed it, and he'd been satisfied with that system since the start. There was only ever one way this could go.

He had always liked it. Before.

He raked his hair back from his face, and wished that he could do something about the way his heart kicked at him. Or better yet, about the fact he had a heart in the first place, despite everything.

Surely if he could rid himself of the thing the way he thought he had a lifetime ago, all of this would be easier.

"I am not going to kill you," he told her, his voice severe as he tried to draw the cloak of his usual remoteness around him. But he couldn't quite get there. "Nonetheless, you have a choice of deaths before you. You can consider this chamber a passageway, of sorts. A bridge between the life you knew until today, and one in which you can be anyone you choose. Assuming you meet the criteria, that is."

She swayed slightly on her feet. "The criteria?"

And he had done this so many times. It should have come as easily to him as breath.

But his chest was too tight. That damned heart of his was too big. "The criteria for escape is simple, Angelina. If you meet it, we will create a new identity for you. You can go anywhere you wish in the world under this new name. You will not have to worry about supporting yourself, because I will take care of your financial arrangements in perpetuity."

"Wait..." Angelina shook her head slightly. "Does that mean...?"

He nodded. "My third wife runs a scuba diving business on an island you would never have heard of, off the coast of Venezuela. My fourth wife lives a nomadic lifestyle, currently traveling about mainland Europe in a converted van. It looks modest from the outside but is, I am assured, the very height of technology within. My fifth wife prefers the frenetic pace of Hong Kong, where she runs a spa. And Veronica, my most famous wife, never able to have a moment to herself in all her days, has settled down on a farm in a temperate valley on the west coast of America. Where she tends to grapes on the vine, raises goats, and makes her own cheese." His smile was a grim and terrible thing. He could taste it. "You can have any life you wish, Angelina. At my expense. All you need to do is disappear forever."

"But if they're not… If you didn't…" She pulled in a visible breath with a ragged sound. "Are you married to all these women at the same time?"

He actually laughed at that. "That is not usually the first question. No, I'm not a bigamist, though I commend you for adding yet another sin to my collection. Murderer and bigamist, imagine! I'm almost sorry to tell you that my marriages have all been quietly and privately annulled. Save the first."

Angelina shifted, hugging herself she stared back at him. "I don't understand. Why would you set yourself up to be some sort of…one-man smuggling operation for women in search of better lives? When you know that the whole world thinks the worst of you?"

"Who better?" Benedetto shrugged. "I don't care in the slightest what the world thinks of me. And you've spent two months acquainting yourself with this castle. It is the tip of the iceberg of the kind of money I have. I could marry a hundred women, support them all, and never feel a pinch in my own pocket."

"So it's altruism then?" She looked dubious, and if he wasn't mistaken, something like… affronted. "If that was true, why not give all that money to charity? Shouldn't there be a way to do it that doesn't brand you the monster beneath every bed in Europe?"

"What would be the fun in that?"

This was the part where normally, the women he'd married—despite their cynicism or inability to trust a word he said because they feared him so deeply, yet not quite deeply enough to refuse to marry him—began to waver. Hope began to creep in. He would watch them imagine, as they stood there before him, that he might be telling them the truth. And if he was, if he could really give them what he was offering, did that mean that they could really, truly be free?

Of him—and of everything else that had brought them here?

But Angelina was staring at him as if what he was telling her was a far worse betrayal than games with his fearsome housekeeper and a key to a locked tower door.

"What do I have to do to qualify for this extraordinary death?" she asked.

He wanted to go to her. He wanted his hands on her. But the point of this, all this, was that Benedetto wasn't supposed to want such things.

He never had before.

"I already told you that the primary purpose of my existence is to produce an heir," he told her stiffly. "It was why I married Carlota and why we planned to consummate a union that was never passionate."

"I remember the story. But that hardly sounds like reason enough to inflict your unhappy childhood on another baby."

"My childhood wasn't unhappy." He heard the outrage in his voice and tried to rein it in. "My grandmother—" But he stopped himself. Because Angelina already knew too much about him. He had already given her too much. Benedetto gritted his teeth and pushed on. "Ordinarily, this is when I offer my wives the opportunity to produce the Franceschi heir themselves."

"Surely they signed up for that when they said, 'I do'?"

He ignored that, and the flash of temper in her blue gaze. "Should you choose that route, life here will continue as is. At the end of a year, if no heir is forthcoming, the same offer for a new life will be made to you. If you're pregnant, however, the expectation would be that you remain until the child is five. At which point, a final offer will be made. If you choose to go, you can do so, with one stipulation. That being, obviously, that you cannot take the child with you. If you choose to stay, we will have contracts drawn up to indicate that you may remain as much a stranger to the marriage as you wish."

He cleared his throat, because this was all standard. This was the labyrinthine game he and his grandfather had crafted and it had served him well for years. But Angelina was staring at him as if he'd turned into an apparition before her very eyes. When this was usually when that sort of gaze faded and a new one took its place. The sweet, bright gleam of *what if.*

"Of course, in your case, everything is different," he said, forcing himself to keep going. "I always leave after the wedding. Usually while they are locked in the bathroom, pretending not to be terrified that I might claim a wedding night. Then I wait to see how long it takes each wife to open the door to this tower. Once she does, we have this discussion."

Again, the way she looked at him was… different.

He cleared his throat. "But your choices might be more limited, regrettably, because you could already be pregnant. I'll confess this has never happened before."

Her lips parted then, and she made a sound that he couldn't quite define. "Are you telling me…? Are you…? Did you not sleep with all your wives on your wedding night? On all your wedding nights?"

"Of course not." He belted that out without thinking. "Nor do I touch them beforehand. I may be considered a monster far and wide, Angelina, but I do *try* not to act like one."

She let out a laugh, a harsh sound against the storm that battered at the windows outside. "Except with me."

Benedetto ran a hand over his face, finding he was only more unsettled as this conversation wore on. Instead of less, as was customary—because he always knew what his wives would choose. He always knew none of them had married *him.* They'd married his money and hoped for the best, and this was him giving it to them.

"The truth is that you were different from the start," he told Angelina, grudgingly. "I had no trouble whatsoever keeping my hands to myself with the rest. It was all so much more…civilized."

He found himself closing the distance between them, when he shouldn't. And he expected her to flinch, but she didn't. She stood her ground, even tilting up her chin, as if she wanted him to do exactly this. As if she wanted him to make it all worse.

Benedetto slid his hand along her cheek, finding it hot and soft, and that didn't solve a single one of his problems. "But you played for me, Angelina. And you wrecked me. And I have been reeling ever since."

Her mouth moved into something far too stark to be a smile. Far too sad to be hers. "That would sound more romantic if you weren't threatening to kill me, one way or another."

"No," he gritted out. "As it happens, you are the only wife I have slept with on a wedding night."

Her eyes seemed remarkably blue then. "What about your second wife? Your mistress? Surely she—"

"She was paralytically drunk after our reception," he said, not sure if that darkness in him was fury, anticipation, or something else he'd never felt before. Something as overwhelming and electric as the storm outside. "And I was little better. I am afraid, Angelina, that you are unique."

"I feel so special," she whispered in that same rough tone, but she didn't jerk her cheek away.

Even so, Benedetto dropped his hand. And for a moment, they stood there, gazing at each other with all these secrets and lies exposed and laid out between them.

He could feel the walls all around him, claiming him anew. For good this time.

When she left him, as he knew she would because they always did, perhaps he would give up the fight altogether. In another year he could be nothing more than another statue, right here in this room. Another stop along the tour.

There was a part of him that longed for the oblivion of stone.

There was a part of him that always would.

"Why?" she asked, her voice a quiet scrape of roughness that reminded him, forcefully, that there was no part of him that was stone. That there never had been, especially where she was concerned. "Why would anyone go to all this trouble?"

"I will answer any and all questions you

might have," he told her, sounding more formal than he intended. Perhaps that was his last refuge. The closest he could get to becoming a statue after all. "But first you must choose."

"As you pointed out, I might already be pregnant," she replied, her arms crossed and even the wildness of her long blond hair a kind of resistance, silver and bright against the bare walls.

Why did he want nothing more than to lose himself in her—forever? How had he let this happen?

"It is true. You might be. I used nothing to prevent it."

"Neither did I. There seemed little need when my life expectancy was all of three months."

And she stared at him, the rebuke like a slap.

He felt it more like a kick to the gut.

"What if I'm pregnant and still choose to disappear tonight?" she asked after a moment, sounding unnervingly calm. "What then? Will you surrender your own child?

Or will you force me to stay here despite the choice I make?"

He shook his head, everything in him going cold. "I told you, you are unique. This has never happened before. That doesn't mean that the possibility is unforeseen. Your choice will hold, no matter your condition."

"You would give up your own child," she murmured. Her eyes widened. "But I thought I was the martyr here."

Benedetto realized his hands were in fists. He didn't know which was worse, that he would have to live without her, which he should have figured out how to handle already, or that it was distinctly possible that she would go off into whatever new life she wished and raise his child without him.

But the rules to this game had been always been perfectly clear.

He and his grandfather had laid them out together.

Half in penance, half for protection. He had already lost two wives. Why not more?

Benedetto had never imagined his heart

would be involved. He'd been certain he'd buried that along with his grandmother.

"You must choose," he gritted out, little as he wanted to.

And for moment, he thought maybe they were dead, after all. Two ghosts running around and around in this terrible castle, cut off from the rest of the world. That the two of them had done this a thousand times before.

Because that was the way she looked at him. As if she'd despaired of him in precisely this way too many times to count already.

He could have sworn he heard her playing then, though there was no piano in sight. Still, the blood in his veins turned to symphonies instead, and he was lit up and lost.

For the first time since he'd started this terrible journey, he honestly didn't know if he could complete it. Or even if he could continue.

And all the while, his seventh wife—and first love, for all the good it would do him in this long, involved exercise in futility—gazed back at him, an expression on her face he'd never seen before.

It made everything in him tighten, like hands around his throat.

"What if I choose a third option instead?" she asked.

Quietly. So very quietly.

Outside, the sea raged and the sky cracked open, again and again. But all he could focus on was Angelina. And those unearthly blue eyes that he was sure could see straight through him and worse, always had.

"There is no third option," he gritted out.

"But of course there is," she said.

And she smiled the way she had when he'd been deep inside her, on that night that shouldn't have happened. The night he couldn't forget.

He heard a great roaring thing and knew, somehow, that it was happening inside him.

"I could stay here," Angelina said with that same quiet strength. "I could have your babies and truly be your wife. No games. No locked towers or forbidden keys. Just you, Benedetto. And me. And whatever children we make between us."

He couldn't speak. The world was a storm,

and he was a part of it, and only Angelina stood apart from it all. A beacon in all the dark.

"We don't have to play games. We don't have to do…whatever this is." Angelina stood there and *shined* at him. He'd never seen that shade of blue before. His heart had never felt so full. "We can do what we want instead."

No one, in the whole of Benedetto's life, had ever looked at him the way she did. As if he was neither her savior nor her hero nor even her worst nightmare. He could have handled any of those. All of them.

But Angelina looked at him as if, should he only allow it, he could be a man.

He didn't know how he stayed on his feet when all he wanted was to collapse to his knees. To beg her to stop. Or to never stop. Or to *think* about what she was doing here.

To him.

"Angelina," he managed to grit out. "You don't know what you're asking."

"But I do." And this time, when her lips curved, it looked like hope. "Benedetto, you asked me to marry you, and I said yes. Now I'm asking you the same thing."

"Angelina..."

"Will you marry me? And better yet—" and her smile widened, and it was all too bright and too much and his chest was cracking open "—will you *stay* married to me? I'm thinking we can start with a long, healthy lifetime and move on from there."

CHAPTER TWELVE

"YOU MUST BE MAD," Benedetto said, his voice strangled.

Angelina couldn't say she wasn't. Maybe the next step was searching out convicted killers and making them her pen pals, as he'd suggested. But she rather thought the only killer who interested her was this one, who'd only ever been convicted in the court of public opinion. And who hadn't killed anyone.

"There is no third option," he said, his voice like gravel. But there was an arrested look on his face that made her heart lurch a bit inside her chest. "I made certain promises long ago. Whether you carry my child now or not is immaterial."

She'd been talking about babies as if she was talking about someone else, but the possibility that it had already happened, that it was happening *even now,* settled on her, then.

She slid a hand over her belly in a kind of wonder. Could it be?

This whole night so far had been like one of her favorite pieces of music. A beautiful journey—a tour of highs and lows, valleys and mountains, storms and sunlight—and all of it bringing her here. Right here.

To this man who was not a monster. No matter how badly he wanted to be.

Her heart had known all along.

"I could do it your way," she said softly. "I could sign up for the heir apparent program. I could keep signing up. We could make it cold-blooded and chilly, if you like. Is that what you want?" There was something so heartbreaking about that, but she knew she would accept it, if it was what he had to offer. She knew she would accept anything if it meant she could have him, even the smallest part of him—but she saw something like anguish on his hard face, then. "Or is it what you think you deserve?"

And for a moment the anguish she could see in him seemed as loud and filled with fury as the storm outside. It was hard to tell which was which—but her heart knew this man. Her heart had recognized him from the start.

It recognized him now.

"It's all right if you can't answer me, Benedetto," she said. She went to him then, stepping close and putting her hands on his chest, where he was as hot to the touch as she recalled. Hotter. She tipped her head back, searching that beautiful, forbidding face of his. "If you can't bring yourself to answer, you don't have to. But tell me how we got here. Tell me why you do all this."

He made a broken sound, this dark, terrible man who was neither of those things.

She didn't understand why she knew it, only that she did. Her heart had known it all along. That was why, though she'd feared for her loneliness and sanity here, she had never truly believed she was in actual, physical danger.

He wasn't any more a butcher than she was. And once that truth had taken hold of her in this empty chamber, all the others swirling around her seemed to solidify. Then fall in behind it like dominoes.

She didn't want to leave him. She didn't want to learn how to scuba dive or to live in a caravan. She didn't want to run a spa in a far-off city, or collect grapes and goats.

She wanted him.

Angelina wanted to look up from her piano to find him studying her, as if she was a piece of witchcraft all her own and only he knew the words to her spell.

Because only he did.

God help her, but she wanted all those things she'd never dared dream about before. Not for the youngest daughter in a family headed for ruin. The one least likely to be noticed and first to be sold off. She wanted *everything.*

"Benedetto," she said again, because it started here. It started with the two of them and this sick game he clearly played not because he wanted to play it, but because he believed he had no other choice. "Who did this to you?"

Then she watched in astonishment as this

big, strong man—this boogeyman feared across the planet, a villain so extreme grown men trembled before him—fell to his knees before her.

"I did this to me," he gritted out. "I did all of this. I am my own curse."

Angelina didn't think. She sank down with him, holding his hands as he knelt there, while all around the tower, the storm outside raged and raged.

The storm in him seemed far more intense.

"Why?" she breathed. "Tell me."

"It was after Sylvia was swept overboard," Benedetto said in a low voice, and the words sounded rough and unused. She didn't need him to tell her that he'd never told this story before. She knew. "You must understand, there was nothing about my relationship with her that anyone would describe as healthy. I should never have married her. As much for her sake as mine."

He stared straight ahead, but Angelina knew he didn't see her. There were too many ghosts in the way.

But she was fighting for a lifetime. She

didn't care if they knelt on the hard stone all night.

She held his hands tighter as he continued.

"Sylvia and I brought out the worst in each other. That was always true, but it was all much sicker after Carlota died. All we did was drink too much, fight too hard, and become less and less able to make up the difference. Then came the storm."

His voice was ravaged. His dark eyes blind. His hands clenched around hers so hard that it might have hurt, had she not been so deeply invested in this moment. In whatever he was about to tell her.

"It took her," Benedetto grated out. "And then I knew what kind of man I was. Because as much as I grieved her, there was a relief in it, too. As if the hand of God reached down and saved me twice, if in horrible ways. Once from a union with a woman I could never make truly happy, because she loved another, and then from a woman who made me as miserable as I made her. The rest of my life, I will have to look in a mirror and know that

I'm the sort of man who thought such things when two women died. That is who I am."

"You sound like a human being," Angelina retorted, fiercely. "If we were all judged on the darkest thoughts that have ever crossed our minds, none of us would ever be able to show our faces in public."

Benedetto shook his head. "My grandfather was less forgiving than you are, Angelina. He called me here, to this castle. He made me stand before him and explain how it was that I was so immoral. So devoid of empathy. Little better than my own father, by his reckoning, given that when my grandmother died he was never the same. He never really recovered." His dark, tortured eyes met hers. "There is nothing he could have said to wound me more deeply."

"Was your father so bad then?" She studied his face. "My own is no great example."

He made a hollow sound. "Your father is greedy. He thinks only of himself. But at least he thinks of *someone*. I don't know how to explain the kind of empty, vicious creature my father was. Only that my grandfather suggesting he and I were the same felt like a death sentence."

"Did you point out that he could always have stepped in himself, then?" Angelina asked, somewhat tartly. "Done a little more parenting than the odd hour on a Sunday? After all, who raised your father in the first place?"

And for moment, Benedetto focused on her instead of the past. She could see it in the way his eyes changed, lightening as he focused on her. In the way that hard mouth of his almost curved in one corner.

"What have I done to earn such ferocity?" he asked, and he sounded almost…humbled.

"You saved me from a selfish man who would have sold me one way or another, if not to you," she said, holding his hands tight. "You gave me a castle. A beautiful piano. And if I'm not very much mistaken, a child, too. What haven't you given me, Benedetto?"

He let out another noise, then reached over, smoothing a hand down over her belly, though it was still flat. She thought of the oddly heightened emotions that had seemed to grip her this last month or so. The strange sensations low in her belly she'd assumed were due to anxiety. She'd felt strange and out of sorts for weeks, and had blamed it on her situation.

But knelt down the hard stone floor of this tower with Benedetto before her, his shoulders wider than the world, she counted back.

And she knew.

Just like that, she knew.

All this time she'd considered herself alone, she hadn't been. Benedetto had been here in the shadows and more, she'd been carrying a part of the both of them deep inside her.

Her heart thumped in her chest, so severely it made her shiver.

"My grandfather reminded me that I have a distant cousin who lives a perfectly unobjectionable life in Brussels. Why should he not leave all this wealth and power to this cousin rather than to me if I found it all so troublesome that I had not only married the most unsuitable woman imaginable, but failed to protect her?" Benedetto shook his head. "He told me that if I wanted to take my rightful place in history, I must subject myself to a test. A test, he made sure to tell me, he did not imagine there was any possibility I would win given my past behavior."

"Did he want you to win?"

He took a moment with that. "All this time I've assumed he wanted to teach me a lesson about loneliness. But I suspect now it was supposed to be a lesson about love."

Benedetto gathered her hands in his again, tugging her closer, and all of this felt like far more important ceremony than the one that had taken place in her father's house. There were no witnesses here but the sky and the sea. The storm. No family members littered about with agendas of their own.

It was only the two of them and the last of the secrets between them.

"My grandfather tasked me with finding women like you," Benedetto said. "Precisely the sort my father had preyed upon, in his time. Women with careless families. Women who might want to run. Women who deserved better than a man with a list of dead wives behind them. I would marry them, but

I would not make them easy about my reputation. I would bring them here. Then I would leave them after the wedding night and let them sit in this castle with all its history and Signora Malandra, who is always only too happy to play her role."

"She's a little too good at her role."

"She, too, always thought I ought to have been a better man," Benedetto said. He shook his head. "When they found their way to this tower I was to offer them a way out. One that kept them safe, gave them whatever they wanted, and made me seem darker and more villainous to the outside world. And he made me vow that I would continue to do this forever, until one of these women gave me a son. And even then, I was to allow her to leave me. Or stay, but live a fully supported, separate life. 'You had two chances and you blew them both,' he told me. 'You don't get any more.'"

"How many chances did he get?" Angelina demanded, her voice as hot as that flash of lightning in her eyes.

"But that was the problem," Benedetto said

in the same way he'd told her, on their wedding night, that he missed the man who had created this prison for him. "My grandfather was a hard man. I do not think he was particularly kind. But he loved my grandmother to distraction and never quite recovered from her loss. She was the best of us. He told me that he was glad she had died before she could see all the ways in which I failed to live up to what she dreamed for me, because after my father had proved so disappointing, they had had such hopes that I would be better."

Angelina frowned. "I'm not sure how you were responsible for Carlota's choices on the one hand—in the face of her own family's pressure, presumably—and an act of nature on the other."

"It was not that I was personally responsible for what happened to them," Benedetto said quietly. "It was that I was so arrogant about both of them. Boorish and self-centered. It never occurred to me to inquire into Carlota's emotional state. And everything Sylvia and I did together was irresponsible. Would a decent man ever have let her out of his sight, knowing the state she was in?"

"A question one could ask of your grandfather," Angelina said.

"But you see, he didn't force me into this. He suggested I bore responsibility and suggested I test myself. I was the one who had spent the happy parts of my childhood playing out involved fantasies in these walls. Ogres and kings. Spells and enchantments. I thought I was already cursed after what had happened to Carlota and Sylvia. Why not prove it? Because the truth is, I never got over the loss of my grandmother either, and she was the one who had always encouraged the games I played. In some twisted way, it seemed like a tribute." Benedetto reached over and touched her face again, smoothing her hair back with one big hand. "And if my grandfather had not agreed, because without her we were both incapable of loving anything—too much like my father—could I have found my way to you?"

She let go the breath she hadn't realized she'd been holding.

"I don't care how you got here," Angelina told him, like another vow. "Just as long as you stay here now you've come."

Outside, lightning flashed and the storm rumbled. The sea fought back.

But inside this tower, empty of everything but the feelings they felt for one another, Angelina felt something bright and big swell up inside her.

It felt like a sob. It felt overwhelming, like grief.

She had the strangest feeling that it was something else altogether.

Something like joy.

"I don't want to leave you," she told him. "I don't want to play these games that serve no one. I have always wanted to be more than a bartering chip for my own father, and you are far more than a monster, Benedetto. What would happen if you and I made our own rules?"

"Angelina…" His voice was a low whisper that she knew, without a shred of doubt, came from the deepest, truest parts of him. "Angelina, you should know. I had read all about the Charteris sisters before I ever came to your father's house. And I assumed that I would pick the one who seemed best suited for me, on paper."

"If you are a wise man," she replied dryly, "you will never tell me which one you mean."

And just like that, both of them were smiling.

As if the sun had come up outside when the rain still fell.

"I walked into that dining room and saw an angel," he told her, wonder in his eyes. In the hands that touched her face. "And I knew better, because I knew that no matter who I chose, it would end up here. Here in the locked tower where all my bodies are buried, one way or another. And still, I looked at you and saw the kind of light I have never believed could exist. Not for me."

"Benedetto..." she whispered, the joy and the hope so thick it choked her.

"I had no intention of touching you, but I couldn't help myself. How could you be anything but an angel, when you could make a piano sing like that? You have entranced me and ruined me, and I have spent two months trying to come to terms with the fact you will leave me like all the rest. I can't."

"You don't have to come to terms with that."

"Maybe this is crazy," he continued, wonder and intensity in every line of his body. "Maybe I'm a fool to imagine that anything that starts in Castello Nero could end well. But I look at you, Angelina, and you make me imagine that anything is possible. Even love, if we do it together."

And for a moment, she forgot to breathe.

Then she did, and the breath was a sob, and there were tears on her face that tasted like the waiting, brooding sea.

Angelina thought, *This is what happiness can be, if you let it.*

If for once she believed in the future before her, not tired old stories of a past she'd never liked all that much to begin with.

If she believed in her heart and her hands, the man before her, and the baby she knew they'd already made.

"Our children will fill these halls with

laughter," she promised him. "And you and I will make love in that bed, where there is nothing but the sea and the sky. It will no more be a chamber of blood, but of life. Love. The two of us, and the good we do. I promise you, Benedetto."

"The sky and the sea are the least of the things I will give you, little one," he vowed in return.

And the stone was cold and hard beneath her, but he was warm. Hot to the touch, and the way he looked at her made her feel as if angels really did sing inside her, after all.

She wrapped herself around him, high up in that tower that she understood, now, wasn't an empty room at all. It was his heart. These stones had only ever held his heart.

Now she would do the honors.

Because she was the seventh wife of the Butcher of Castello Nero. The first one to love him, the only one to survive intact, and soon enough the mother of his children besides.

There was no storm greater than the way she planned to love this man.

Deeper and longer than the castle itself could stand—and it had lasted centuries already.

And she started here, on the floor of this tower, where he settled her on top of him and gazed up at her as if she was the sun.

And then, together, moment by moment and year by year, they both learned how to shine.

Bright enough to scare away the darkest shadows.

Even the ones they made themselves.

Forever.

CHAPTER THIRTEEN

THE SEVENTH WIFE of the terrifying Butcher of Castello Nero confounded the whole world by living.

She lived, and well, by all accounts. She appeared in public on Benedetto's arm and gave every appearance of actually enjoying her husband's company. As months passed, it became apparent that she was expecting his child, and that, too, sent shock waves across the planet.

The tabloids hardly knew what to do with themselves.

And as the years passed without the faintest hint of blood or butchery, Benedetto found himself becoming something he'd never imagined he could. Boring.

Beautifully, magnificently boring to the outside world, at last.

Their first child, a little boy they called

Amadeo to celebrate some of the music that had bound them to each other, thrived. When he was four, he was joined by a little brother. Two years later, a sister followed. And a year after that, another little girl joined the loud, chaotic clan in the castle on its tidal island.

A place only Angelina had seemed to love the way he always had, deny it though he might.

And Benedetto's children were not forced to secrete themselves in hidden places, kept out of sight from tourist groups, or permitted only a weekly hour with him. Nor were they sent off to boarding school on their fifth birthdays. His children raced up and down the long hallways, exactly as Angelina had said they would. The stone walls themselves seemed lighter with the force of all that laughter and the inevitable meltdowns, and the family wing was soon anything but lonely. There was an endless parade between the nursery at one end, the master suite on the other, and all the rooms in between.

Ten years to the day that Benedetto had brought his last, best wife home, he stood at that wall of windows that looked out over the sea, the family wing behind him. He knew that even now, the staff was setting up something romantic for the two of them in that empty tower room that they kept that way deliberately.

Because it reminded them who they were.

And because it was out of reach of even their most enterprising child, because Angelina still wore the key he'd left her around her neck.

They would put the children to sleep, reading them stories and hearing their prayers, and then they would walk down this very same hall the way they always did. Hand in hand. The bloodred ruby on her hand no match for the fire inside him.

The fire he would share with her up there where they had pledged themselves to each other. The fire that only grew over time.

Benedetto was not the villain he'd played. He was not the boogeyman, as so many would no doubt believe until he died no matter what he did.

But any good in him, he knew with every

scrap of conviction inside him, came from his angel. His wife and lover, who he had loved since the very first moment he'd laid eyes on her. The mother of his perfect, beautiful, never remotely disappointing children. The woman who had reminded him of the child he'd been—the child who had believed in all the things he'd had to relearn.

And the best piano player he had ever had the privilege of hearing.

He could hear her playing now, the notes soaring down from the tower that was still hers. These days, there was often art taped to the walls, and the children lay on the rug before the grand piano so they could be near her. So they could feel as if they were flying, too, as their mother played and played, songs of hope, songs of love. Songs of loss and recovery.

And always, always, songs of joy.

These were the spells she cast, he thought. These were her enchantments.

The sun began to sink toward the horizon. Pinks and reds took over the sky. And still she played, and he could picture her so perfectly, bent over the keys with her eyes half closed. Her hands like magic, coaxing so much beauty out into the world.

He could hardly wait to have them on him again, where he liked them best.

Benedetto had so many things to tell her, the way he always did after time apart. Whether it was five minutes or five weeks. How much he loved her, for one thing. How humbled he still was, a decade on, that she had seen the good in him when it had been hidden from everyone. Even himself.

Especially himself.

She had a heart as big as the sea, his lovely wife. She maintained a relationship with her family, and he rather thought her quiet example made her sisters strive to be better than they might otherwise have been. Her mother, too, in those few and far between moments Margrete Charteris thawed a little. And if her father could never really be saved, it hardly mattered. Because Anthony Charteris had as a son-in-law a rich and besotted billionaire more than willing to spend his money on his father-in-law if it pleased his wife.

After all, there was always more money.

Benedetto would spend it all if it made her happy.

He heard the music stop and found himself smiling. He decided he would wait until they were alone to tell her that he had decided to share her piano playing with the world. Whether she wanted to perform or not, he could certainly share her music. He thought the world deserved to know that not only had Angelina soothed the savage beast with her playing, she was one of the best in the world. Accordingly, he'd bought her a record company.

But that would come.

First there was tonight.

He heard her feet on the stone and then she was there beside him, her eyes still the bluest he'd ever seen. Particularly when they were sparkling with music and love and light, and all of it for him.

"Happy anniversary, little one," he murmured, kissing her. He felt that same rush of longing and lust, desire and need, tempered now with these long, sweet years. "I have loved you each and every day. I love you now. And I only plan to love you more."

"I'm delighted to hear that," she replied, in that dry way he adored. "I love you too. And it turns out I have a rather bigger gift for you than planned."

Benedetto turned to look at her in some surprise, and Angelina smiled.

She took his hand in hers—her thumbs moving over the calluses there that it had taken her years to understand he got from performing the acts of physical labor he preferred to a gym membership—and moved it to her belly.

And he had done this so many times before. It was the same surge of love and wonder, sweetness and hope. Disbelief that she could make him this happy. Determination to do it better than his parents had, no matter what it took.

He was already better, he liked to think. If his grandmother could see him now, he was sure he would make her smile. And maybe even his grandfather, too.

“Again?” he asked, grinning wide enough to crack his own jaw.

“We really should do something about it,” she said, her eyes shining. “It’s almost unseemly. But… I just don’t want to.”

He pulled her to him, marveling as ever at how perfectly and easily she fit in his arms. “Angelina, my angel, if you wish to have enough children to fill this entire castle, we will make it so.”

She laughed, her mouth against his. “Let’s not get *that* carried away.”

And he kissed her, because the future was certain.

That wasn’t to say he knew what would happen, because no man could. Storms came. Sometimes they took more than was bearable. Sometimes they left monsters in their wake.

But he was not alone anymore.

He had Angelina, and together, they made their own light. And Benedetto knew that no matter how dark it became, they would find a way to light it. And with that light, they would find their way through.

They would always find their way through.

And all the while they would stay here, in this ancient place where they'd found each other. When the tide was low, they would welcome in the world. There would be laughter in the halls, and deliciously creepy stories about disappearances both centuries old and more recent.

But soon enough the tide would come in, and the castle would be theirs again.

Like their heart made stone and cared for throughout time, they would love this place. They would love each other and their children. They would choose light over dark, hope over heartache, and they would do what no other Franceschi ever had across the ages.

They would make Castello Nero a home.

Their home.

And he kissed her again, long and deep, because that was how forever happened when it was made of love—one life-altering kiss at a time.

* * * * *

1 2 3 4 5 6 7 8 11 12 13 14 15
17 26 28 29 30